"Fraternizing with a guest...

...will surely be frowned upon by my new employer. I didn't think acting on the attraction would be wise." She saw some subtle shift in his expression. "I still don't," she rushed to add.

"Nevertheless." He shifted closer, his right hand grazing her jaw to lift her chin. "I'd like to test the truth of that claim."

"That I don't think we should act on it?" Her breathless voice sounded nothing like her.

"That you're attracted to me." His thumb skimmed along her lower lip and pleasure trembled through her even though she tried to hold herself very still.

He broke away suddenly. For a moment, she was utterly disoriented, blinking back at him in the glow of the barn light overhead. His hands lingered on her back.

"The chemistry is real enough." He didn't seem in any hurry to release her. "But is your story?"

* * *

The Rival is part of the Dynasties: Mesa Falls series.

Dear Reader,

Having raised three sons of my own, I love a brother story. Devon Salazar may think he doesn't get along with his sibling, but, as a mom, I can tell you that I was rooting for them to mend fences from the start.

Of course, Devon's bigger concern is solving the mystery of Regina Flores—a woman with too many secrets. I hope you enjoy this return to Mesa Falls Ranch, where a scandal is brewing!

If you enjoy this story, I hope you will join me in February for Weston Rivera's book.

Happy reading!

Joanne Rock

JOANNE ROCK

THE RIVAL

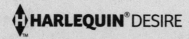
HARLEQUIN® DESIRE

To the new bride Susan Newkirk Heath,
who shares my romantic streak.

ISBN-13: 978-1-335-60405-7

The Rival

Copyright © 2019 by Joanne Rock

PLEASE RECYCLE
THIS PRODUCT IS RECYCLABLE

Recycling programs
for this product may
not exist in your area.

HARLEQUIN®
www.Harlequin.com

Printed in U.S.A.

Joanne Rock credits her decision to write romance after a book she picked up during a flight delay engrossed her so thoroughly that she didn't mind at all when her flight was delayed two more times. Giving her readers the chance to escape into another world has motivated her to write over eighty books for a variety of Harlequin series.

Visit her Author Profile page at Harlequin.com, or joannerock.com, for more titles.

You can also find Joanne Rock on Facebook, along with other Harlequin Desire authors, at Facebook.com/harlequindesireauthors!

Mesa Falls

The Key Players

Mesa Falls Ranch, Montana's premier luxury corporate retreat, got its start when a consortium bought the property.

The Owners

Weston Rivera, rancher

Miles Rivera, rancher

Gage Striker, investment banker

Desmond Pierce, casino resort owner

Alec Jacobsen, game developer

Jonah Norlander, technology company CEO

What do the owners have in common?

They all went to Dowdon School, where they were students of the late Alonzo Salazar.

The Salazars

Alonzo Salazar (dec.), retired teacher at Dowdon School, CEO of Salazar Media

Devon Salazar, copresident, Salazar Media, Alonzo's son

Marcus Salazar, copresident, Salazar Media, Alonzo's son, Devon's half brother

As these key players converge, dark secrets come to light in Big Sky Country...

Where family loyalties and passions collide...

One

As she worked in the tack room at Mesa Falls Ranch, Regina Flores caught sight of her reflection in a shiny halter plate bearing one of the horse's names. Even six months after her makeover, it still surprised her sometimes to see another woman's face staring back at her.

Bypassing the fancy dress tack, Regina chose an everyday bridle and rushed back to the stable to finish saddling a second mount. She'd wheedled her way onto the ranch staff as a trail guide the week before and still hadn't found an opportunity to get close to Devon Salazar, whose company was overseeing the social media marketing and launch event for the ranch's rebranding as a private corporate retreat. Getting close to Devon was the only reason she'd taken the job. And she never could have accomplished that if she'd borne any resemblance to her old self—Georgiana Fuentes.

Tightening the saddle girth on the second horse, Regina finished tacking up quickly before unhooking the crossties. She brought both horses through the paddock area before mounting her own and leading the second. She'd heard Devon had a meeting coming up at the main lodge and there was a chance she could talk him into riding there with her. But only if she hurried.

She nudged the bay mustang faster until the main buildings were out of sight. The ranch owners had given Devon a two-bedroom cabin right on the Bitterroot River, a more remote property with beautiful views and a multilevel deck to take in the sights. She'd made careful notes about all the ranch's buildings in order to land the trail guide job. Regina had sacrificed everything to be here now—for this chance to learn the truth about the Salazar heirs.

How much did Devon Salazar know about the book his dead father had penned under a pseudonym eight years ago? A tell-all that had caused life as she'd known it to implode? She'd overheard him deny all knowledge of it to his brother in a conversation last week, but she'd also learned the siblings didn't trust each other, so she didn't put much stock in what he'd told Marcus.

Her private investigator had only recently discovered the identity of the author—two months *after*

Alonzo Salazar's death—so she'd had to transfer her need for revenge from the father to the sons. Because she didn't believe for a second that they hadn't benefited from their father's decision to unmask her family's secrets for financial gain.

A light snow began to fall as she guided the horses off the trail to a shortcut that would bring her to Devon's cabin faster.

She should be thankful she bore no resemblance to the woman she used to be. If she'd still looked anything like sweet, innocent Georgiana Fuentes, Devon might have recognized her as one of the thinly disguised real-life characters in his dad's supposed work of "fiction." Or, more accurately, from the endless images of her in the press after a Hollywood gossip columnist had linked the novel's characters to their real-life counterparts.

But stress had stolen thirty pounds from her frame. Relentless workouts in an effort to excise her anger had sculpted a much different body from the soft curves of her teenage self. Even worse, being hounded by the tabloids for her story had caused a car accident three years ago that required enough facial reconstruction to alter her features. Finally, to complete the transformation, six months ago, she'd hacked off her long blond waves to just above her shoulders and dyed the remaining hair a deep chocolate brown. Regina had effectively scrubbed away every last remnant of the woman she used to be.

Devon would never guess she'd once been the spoiled heiress of a powerful A-list actor who'd disowned her and her mother when he learned that Georgiana wasn't his biological daughter, thanks to the tell-all book. She'd done therapy for her anger issues with her family long ago. But she'd then realized she couldn't really start building a new life until she understood why her old one had been taken from her.

And whether or not Devon and Marcus Salazar had profited from the book that had cost her everything.

Leaning back in the saddle, she slowed the lead horse just before Devon's cabin came into view. She needed to brace herself mentally for seeing the man who had almost assuredly built his business empire thanks to her misfortune. He was her enemy.

So it threw her that he was absurdly handsome. His green eyes had sparked an unwelcome heat inside her the only time she'd spoken to him two days ago, when she'd invited him on a trail ride.

Being around him rattled her, but she had to hide it. Had to stay focused. Because she would do whatever was necessary to uncover the truth.

"You're leaving?" Standing in the living area of his two-bedroom cabin on the Mesa Falls Ranch property, Devon Salazar glared at his half brother, Marcus, knowing he shouldn't be surprised by the news.

When had they ever seen eye to eye on anything?

They'd only come to the ranch to honor a deathbed promise to their father before his passing. Because even though they ran a company together, they did so from offices on opposite coasts—Devon in New York and Marcus in Los Angeles. Devon had assumed their father wanted them to spend time in the same place so they would work out their differences and settle the future of Salazar Media. Little did he know Alonzo Salazar had only called them there to drop a bombshell on them, which they discovered in the paperwork he'd left with the ranch owners before his death.

"I know the timing is unfortunate," Marcus conceded, prowling around the living area in a dark blue suit, his sunglasses still perched on his head from when he'd shown up at Devon's cabin twenty minutes ago. His only nod to the fast-dropping Montana temperatures was the wool scarf slung around his neck. "But Lily and I have left you a thorough plan for the launch event. All you need to do is execute it."

Barely hanging onto his patience, Devon stared out at the densely forested mountainside just beyond his luxury cabin's tiered deck.

"All I need to do is execute?" he repeated, glaring at the sea of ponderosa pines just beyond the big windows. He hadn't been brought up to speed on the client yet, and most of the ranch owners—it was jointly held by six friends—were still aggravated with Devon for showing up more than a week late at the ranch and delaying the work on the relaunch. "While you and Lily gallivant around Europe for a few weeks?"

Marcus had fallen in love with the COO of Salazar Media, Lily Carrington. While Devon had delayed his trip to Montana to hire a private investigator to look more deeply into their father's mysterious past, Marcus had been at the ranch wooing the woman Devon had sent in his absence. Losing both of them during the launch event for a new, prestigious client was a hard hit.

"We did the setup. Now it's your turn," Marcus explained, his usual antagonism noticeably absent. Maybe romance agreed with him. "Besides, I'm hoping this trip turns into an elopement," he confided, the announcement a total surprise.

Knowing what a difficult—and long—engagement Lily had to her previous fiancé, Devon could see the wisdom of that move. Some of his anger leaked away. He and his half brother might not get along, but Devon wanted Lily to be happy. Hell, he didn't begrudge Marcus being happy, either.

"You haven't asked her yet?"

Marcus shook his head. "No. I was thinking of surprising her in Paris. Pulling out all the stops."

"That's a good idea, actually." Funny to think their shared business—and a shared father—had never brought them together, but if Marcus married Lily, they might finally have an effective tie. "I only want what's best for her, you know."

"I know." His sibling's dark eyes met his for a moment before he glanced away. "And so do I. She hasn't taken a vacation in years. She deserves for someone to put her first."

Devon didn't need to be reminded of the particulars. Lily had been raised to feel like an intruder in her grandparents' wealthy world and she'd worked tirelessly to feel deserving of all they'd done for her. Their backgrounds weren't all that different, since Devon's single mother had moved back in with her old-money family after Alonzo Salazar had abandoned her shortly after Devon's birth.

"Agreed." He would find a way to make the launch event work on his own. He would bring in more staff, for starters. "But you realize the bigger issue right now is not the launch, but trying to contain the fallout from whatever new scandal Dad's book could cause."

Hammering out an agreement for the future of Salazar Media—and who would take the helm of the business—would have to wait.

"But for now, no one knows about that. If the secret comes out somehow, we'll deal with it when it happens," Marcus assured him, checking his watch. "In the meantime, I've got to pick up Lily so we can head to the airstrip. We're flying out this afternoon."

Devon resisted the urge to argue. The ramifications of the secret leaking out were bigger than they knew. But Marcus had been the one to nail down the ranch as a client, and he'd kept the situation under control with the owners until Devon had arrived, so he'd done his part. Now Devon would have to find a way to keep any revelations about their father's book from ruining everything they'd both worked so hard for.

"Good luck," he told him simply, extending a hand.

Marcus stared down at it for a beat too long, but

he squeezed Devon's palm in the end. "Thank you. And you'd better get moving if you want to make that meeting with Weston Rivera. It's almost noon."

Devon swore as he shoved his phone in his pocket and headed toward the coatrack to retrieve a fitted black parka. "I won't bother you unless all hell breaks loose."

"I can give you a ride over there—"

"No need." The main lodge was in the opposite direction from Marcus's cabin. "You added the ranch to our client list. I'll make the rest of it work."

His brother gave a clipped nod before stepping out into the December chill, a burst of cold air lingering in his wake when he closed the door.

Devon shut his laptop and hunted down a hat and a pair of gloves, already mulling over how he was going to juggle orchestrating the kickoff party with digging deeper into their father's secrets. He hadn't wanted to share with Marcus his own reasons for needing to keep the Salazar dirty laundry out of the headlines for at least two more weeks. Devon's socialite mother was set to wed an international banker on Christmas Eve in a highly publicized ceremony. She had found happiness at last, and Devon refused to let a scandal about his father overshadow her well-deserved spotlight.

Maybe Devon's paranoia about his father's secrets leaking now were misplaced, considering Alonzo had kept his double life as an author on lockdown for eight years. But Devon's gut told him that his dad's death was going to bring everything to light.

The papers Alonzo had left for his sons here at the ranch revealed all the details. Under the pseudonym A. J. Sorensen, Alonzo had released an international bestselling novel about Hollywood power brokers and scandals. The book had caused an uproar a year after its release, when a Beverly Hills gossip columnist cracked the code on the identities of the people who inspired the characters.

Real people had been hurt by the book. A Hollywood marriage had been torn apart. A daughter disowned.

Devon pulled a gray knit cap over his ears and tugged open the cabin door just as a light snow began to fall. He spotted a woman on horseback heading toward him. She had a dark Stetson pulled low on her forehead, and it was difficult to see her features through the swirl of snowflakes, but Devon recognized her as the trail guide employed by Mesa Falls Ranch. She'd approached him two days ago about taking a tour of the property to familiarize him with the ranch, an idea he might have jumped on another time, but he'd been reeling from the news about his father's secrets.

Regina Flores had made an impression, though.

With her silver-gray eyes and dark hair, she'd captured his attention right away. She had a thoughtful, brooding air about her; she seemed to be a woman of deep, mysterious thoughts. Until she smiled. She had a mischievous, quick grin that made him think wholly inappropriate things. Today she wore a black duster that flared over her horse's saddle and a purple scarf tied around her neck. She held the reins to a second mount, a sturdy chestnut quarter horse.

"Hello, Mr. Salazar." She flashed a smile his way, two deep dimples framing her lips as she drew to a stop in front of the cabin.

He wasn't a man easily distracted by physical attraction, but something about this woman's ease in her own skin called to him in spite of his looming worries. It made him very aware of how long it had been since he'd shared his bed. He'd been so focused on growing the company he hadn't made time for anything but the most fleeting encounters over the past two years.

"Good morning." He stepped down the deck steps to ground level as the snowfall began picking up speed. "And call me Devon."

Her mustang whinnied a greeting, shaking its mane. Devon stopped near the horse's head to stroke the muzzle, noting the flurries melting on its nose. Safer to look the animal in the eye than its appealing rider.

"I heard from Mr. Rivera that the two of you have a meeting, so I thought I'd offer you a lift." She jutted her chin in the direction of the chestnut mare behind her. "Nutmeg is saddled and ready to go if you are."

"You came all the way out here on the off chance I'd need a ride?" His gaze skimmed up her denim-clad thigh, over her feminine curves, to study her expression. Was there a chance Regina Flores felt the same pull he did when they were near one another?

The idea revved him up.

"I didn't have any trail rides scheduled for today and both these animals were due for some exercise, so my offer isn't quite as generous as you make it sound." Her smile was self-deprecating this time. "I had to get Nutmeg out either way."

She might well be telling the truth.

But the alternative—that she harbored a personal interest in him—was far more intriguing. Especially during a tense week, with his business hanging in the balance. He could see the potential benefit of a distraction.

"To tell you the truth, I'd be grateful for the company," he said at last, reaching up to take Nutmeg's reins from Regina.

He briefly caught her hand in his, leather on leather, before sliding the horse's lead free.

Regina's quicksilver eyes tracked him, her smile fleeing as awareness flickered between them. At least, he'd like to think that she'd felt it, too.

"Do you need a hand up?" she asked even as he slung a leg over Nutmeg's back.

"I'll be fine." He urged the chestnut forward two steps so he was beside Regina.

Close enough to touch.

"Suit yourself." Her gaze darted around, as if unsure where to land. "Just keep in mind some of our horses are more spirited than others. It's a good idea to get acquainted with their quirks first."

"In that case, anything I need to know about Nutmeg?" He was far more interested in getting to know the trail guide than the gentle mare.

"She's a follower." Regina shifted in the saddle and her horse eased back a step from his. "She'll be more comfortable letting me take the lead."

"Fair enough." He opened his hand with the reins still balanced on his palm, giving the horse her lead. "But since I'm most definitely not a follower, next time feel free to give me something feistier." He allowed his words to sink in before leaning fractionally closer. "I like a challenge."

Her swift intake of breath, a soft and sexy gasp, was the most pleasant sound he'd heard in days.

And just like that, he had something to look forward to during an otherwise hellish week. Regina Flores was a welcome feminine distraction when all the rest of his world was falling apart.

Pull it together.

Regina cursed herself for finding anything remotely attractive about a man she knew to be her enemy.

Tall and leanly muscled, Devon carried himself with athletic grace in dark jeans and a fitted black parka. A gray ski cap covered his light brown hair, the knit fabric framing thick eyebrows and pale green eyes. With sculpted features, he was handsome in a way that should have been boringly traditional. Except there was something undeniably compelling about the way his eyes followed her. He didn't seem like the kind of man who paid attention to every random woman in his field of vision. She'd had time to observe him unnoticed, and he was normally all business. Yet, around her, she felt the heated spark of masculine interest.

She put the bay in motion. The hoofbeats were softened by the layer of snow sticking on the trail back to the main lodge at Mesa Falls Ranch. The wind picked up, swirling flakes that tickled her cheeks. She appreciated the icy kiss on her skin, needing something to cool her frustration.

Her keen awareness.

She'd worked too hard to get close to him to lose focus now. Her whole point in bringing Devon a mount had been to talk to him. Earn his confidence. Instead, the moment he'd gotten close to her, she'd felt the most bizarrely unexpected reaction to him.

Blatant physical attraction.

It would have been unsettling enough if it had been one-sided. But Devon's comment about liking a challenge hadn't only been about the horses.

Breathing out slowly, she told herself to let go of the moment and focus on salvaging this time with Devon. His younger brother and business partner, Marcus, was leaving the ranch today with the COO of Salazar Media, Lily Carrington. The pair had fallen in love and spent so much time together during their stay at Mesa Falls Ranch that Regina had had no opportunity to get near Marcus.

Devon was her last chance to find out how much the Salazar family knew about their father's book. She'd risked her cover to eavesdrop on a conversation between the brothers the week before, enough to learn that Marcus and Devon didn't trust each other at all even though they were business partners. And that fact alone called into question everything that had transpired between them.

They'd spoken like they didn't know about their father's book. But could one—or both—of them have been lying?

One thing was certain: she wasn't going to learn any more if she didn't try to get to know Devon better.

Slowing her horse's step, she waited until he was close to her again. She noticed he allowed her to keep the lead, however.

"You ride very well," she observed lightly, daring a glance toward him as they followed the Bitterroot River toward the lodge. "Did you grow up around horses?"

He stared out through the snow-covered field where a few deer picked their way back into a thicket.

"Not really. I went to school with a guy who lived on a Kentucky Thoroughbred farm and I spent a couple of summers with his family." He pointed toward the woods where the deer had disappeared. "Look. The fawn wants to come back and play."

Sure enough, the smallest of the deer hopped out into the field again, running in a circle before it darted back into the trees in a flash of white tail. She felt herself smiling along with Devon until she remembered she had to keep up her guard.

"Now that I know what a strong rider you are, I'm all the more determined to take you out on one of the trails while you're here." She figured a little flattery couldn't hurt her cause. "You must want to see the full spread of the ranch while you're preparing for the launch party?"

"I do." He turned those pale green eyes her way, his expression serious. "As long as you're my guide."

Her heart pounded harder.

Only because she was circling the enemy, damn it. She ground her teeth together. *Focus.*

"Deal." She forced a smile as they rounded the last bend before the main lodge came into view. "Name a time. I actually need to put in more trail ride hours myself, familiarize myself with the place, before Mesa Falls Ranch opens to the corporate retreats at the end of the month."

"How's tomorrow morning?" His breath huffed a cloud in the cold air as he spoke. "I can clear my calendar and spend the day taking in the sights."

"Excellent." She'd have Devon all to herself. Surely she'd find out something about his father and what kind of relationship Devon had with the man who'd used Regina's family secrets to make a fortune. "Should I meet you at your cabin?"

"I'll come to the stables." He nudged Nutmeg in the flank, turning her toward the lodge. "You can help me choose the right mount."

"Of course." She wondered if his knowledge of horses was better than hers. She'd had to exaggerate her skills a bit to land the trail guide job. "We can have the kitchen pack us a meal if you think we'll stay out through the lunch hour."

"Absolutely." Devon nodded. "I had a lot on my

plate when you first mentioned the idea of a trail ride, but I'll be ready to give you my full attention tomorrow." Slowing his horse to a halt, he let his gaze linger on Regina. "In fact, I look forward to it."

She stared back at him for a moment too long, trying to read the undercurrent between them. Trying to ignore the pull of attraction.

"Sounds good," she said finally, needing to stay polite. Professional. Friendly.

No matter that her feelings for him veered between suspicion and simmering awareness.

Dismounting, he turned to stride into the lodge for his meeting, leaving Regina to bring Nutmeg back to the stables. She watched him walk away, his dark boots leaving an imprint as he charged through the coating of powdery snow.

Tomorrow, he'd promised her his undivided attention. That had potential for her investigation into what the Salazar heirs knew about their father's activities. But he'd also made it clear he was interested in her, and that complicated things considerably. For some reason she was okay deceiving him about her identity, but not okay using the attraction between them as some sort of bargaining chip.

She'd have to find a way to get the answers she needed without succumbing to the draw of the man.

And even after spending only ten minutes with Devon Salazar, she knew that wasn't going to be easy. But failure wasn't an option. One way or another, Regina would find out where the profits from Alonzo Salazar's book were going. If it turned out

Devon Salazar had benefited financially from the wreckage of her world?

She would use everything in her power to make sure he paid.

Two

Regina stayed up late and awoke early, wanting to ensure she was well prepared for the outing with Devon. She had studied everything she might possibly need to know for the trail ride—weather conditions, interesting sights along the way, a refresher on the native plants and animals. She'd also spent some time rehearsing a few basic details of her cover story since she couldn't reveal anything personal for fear of giving away her past as Georgiana.

Now she was huddled inside the barn, checking the map on her phone so she didn't get lost during the ride, when Devon arrived.

"Morning." The deep masculine voice warmed

her insides even before she turned to see him standing under the arch of the doorway.

Snow stirred behind him in a misty white cloud as he pulled on a pair of leather gloves. From his jeans and boots to his dark sheepskin jacket, he looked ready for the outing and not at all like her idea of a Manhattan executive. Straightening, she tucked her phone in the pocket of her jacket.

"Good morning, Devon." She forced a smile in spite of the weird mixture of nervousness and tamped-down attraction. "Are you ready to ride?"

"I've been eagerly anticipating this." His green eyes lingered on her as he stepped deeper into the barn. "And I hope you don't mind, but I took the liberty of making a few adjustments to the lunch you ordered from the kitchen."

He held up a sleekly packaged parcel that she hadn't noticed he was carrying.

"Perfect." She'd been planning to stop by the kitchen on their way out. She opened one of the saddlebags. "You can slide it in here."

He was by her side in a few steps, the heat and warmth of him blocking the cold air blowing in through the open doors.

He smelled like pine trees and soap. A fact she wished she hadn't noticed. He stepped back from the Appaloosa.

"I see you saddled a different mount for me today." He patted the mare's flank while she closed the flap on the saddlebag.

"I know you hoped for something more spirited. Your brother was partial to Evangeline," she told him smoothly, pretending not to know anything about their enmity. "I thought maybe you'd enjoy her, too."

Leading his horse out of the barn, he gave a humorless laugh. "Marcus and I have rarely agreed on anything, but I won't hold that against Evangeline."

A few moments later, they were mounted and trotting away from the barns at a good clip. Regina tipped her face up into the falling snow, enjoying the fresh air and the beauty of Big Sky Country despite the rider beside her. She found it difficult to relax around him, given her overwhelming need to learn more about his connection to his father and the book that had destroyed her life. But at least his remark about Marcus had given her a toehold into that conversation.

Her cheeks tingled with the chill of the icy snow as she began her most basic introduction to Mesa Falls Ranch, outlining the size and rough parameters of the place, skimming over the ownership, since she assumed Devon knew all about the unique group who managed the property.

"Have you met all of the owners?" Devon asked as they began the steep trek out of Bitterroot Valley.

"I haven't." She hadn't really understood the point of the shared ranch venture. Most ranches were either family owned or held by a major corporation. Yet Mesa Falls was owned equally by six friends who had never made the bottom line a primary concern. "I've only met Weston Rivera, who spends the most time on site overseeing things." She pointed to a break in the trees ahead. "We'll be able to see his house from just up there."

"I've been to his home. I got to meet a few of the owners at a welcome party they threw at Rivera's place last week." Devon appeared more relaxed than he had the day before, even though his mount was definitely more energetic.

For her part, Regina felt on edge, wanting to remain alert to any clues he might give her about his family, his business and his sources of income.

Swaying with the mustang's movements, she debated the best way to broach those topics.

"I remember hearing about that. Your brother went, too, I think." She knew a lot about Marcus's movements even though she hadn't spoken to him directly. Last week, she'd still been feeling her way around the ranch after landing the job. She'd spied on Marcus more than once.

"He did." Devon's answer was clipped.

"The two of you have a business together, and yet you mentioned you don't see eye to eye on many things." She glanced his way to gauge his expression. "Doesn't that make working together difficult?"

"Absolutely," he said without hesitation. "Thankfully, we have offices on opposite coasts, and that helps."

She wanted to ask a follow-up question but didn't want to sound like she was interrogating him. So she waited.

"Do you have siblings, Regina?" he asked as they cleared a rise. The terrain leveled off slightly as the horses picked their way along the narrow trail under the shelter of the pines.

"No." That wasn't strictly true since she had two half siblings, her father's kids she'd never been allowed to meet. Her birth father's wife was highly protective of her family, resenting Regina's late appearance in their lives. "I've always envied people with bigger families."

Families that didn't disown their children.

Birds squawked in the trees overhead, their movements causing more snow to rain down on them as they disturbed the branches.

"Marcus and I didn't spend any time together growing up," Devon explained as they left the trees behind and arrived on a plateau above the river. "Our mothers viewed one another as rivals, so Marcus and I did, too."

"Yet you started a very successful business together."

He looked sharply at her. "You've done your homework."

Her cheeks heated; yes, she had dug through everything she could find about Salazar Media. Especially since Devon's father had been a part owner. "You and Marcus are the first guests since I've been a trail guide. I figured it doesn't hurt to know who I'm talking to."

"I'm flattered," he admitted. "I'm usually the one

doing all the studying about new clients. I can't remember the last time anyone tried to impress me."

His gaze collided with hers and she felt the prickle of awareness all over her skin, even with the cold wind blowing off the mountains. Her mouth dried up as she debated how to respond. Thankfully, he had questions about their direction and the next two hours passed uneventfully enough.

She kept up a running patter about the sights, the history of the Bitterroot River, and the best spots for fly-fishing according to the locals she'd asked. They were far from the main ranch house when she spotted a creek side lean-to that one of the ranch hands had told her about. Built by one of the owners for a winter retreat, the lean-to was open on one side, with a picnic table tucked under the shelter.

"Are you ready for lunch?" she asked, shifting in the saddle to see Devon better. "There's a good spot to make a fire by the water if you want one."

She could see the fire ring between the lean-to and the creek, the spot sheltered from the wind.

"Sounds good." He followed her down the snowy hill to the open hut with its bark and branch roof.

She settled the horses close to the water while Devon unpacked the food. She found a few promising sticks to build a fire, kicked away the excess snow, then got to work starting a blaze. By the time she turned around, Devon had flannel blankets on both benches, a clean linen over the table and two glasses of wine poured into stemless glasses. A centerpiece of bread, meats and cheeses was surrounded by fruit, nuts and even a small jar of honey.

With the fire snapping behind her, the flames giving the winter picnic a burnished glow, things had taken a turn for the romantic.

"Wow." She darted her gaze to his, not sure what to say. "That definitely looks better than the turkey sandwiches I asked the staff chef to make us."

He waved her closer. "I hope you don't mind. But I like to combine work with pleasure whenever I can, and Montana is too beautiful not to savor."

Her heartbeat jumped nervously as she neared him to slide onto one of the bench seats. She needed to be wary of this man's idea of pleasure. She had too much at stake to lose focus now.

"Of course," she tried to say in a normal tone, but her voice cracked like a twelve-year-old boy's. She cleared her throat and tried again. "It's a treat for me, too."

"I'm glad." He took the seat opposite her and waited while she removed her gloves and filled a plate for herself. "So how long have you worked here?"

She took a sip of her wine to steel herself for the inevitable questions and hoped she could change the topic fast.

"I just started last week. I'm having a hard time deciding on a career path since I finished college, so I've been testing out different jobs, trying to figure out what I want to do and where I'd like to live." It was close enough to the truth.

She didn't mention that she couldn't properly get her life underway until she had the answers she needed about A. J. Sorensen's book and where all the profits from it had gone.

"Really?" Devon stretched his long legs under the table, one knee bumping hers. "Where did you attend college?"

"Online." That wasn't true. She'd taken most of her classes on the UCLA campus—right up until her accident. "It was easier that way, since I enjoy moving around."

"And where's home?" he asked, dipping a corner of the fresh bread into the honey.

"My mother lives in Tahoe." That was true. "I guess home is there." Technically, Regina had only ever visited for a couple of days at a time.

Her mother had left Hollywood as soon as she could after the scandal broke, but Regina had remained in Los Angeles with her grandmother to finish high school. At the time, she couldn't imagine living without her friends, but one by one her friends had all fallen away after the scandal. Even Terri, her best friend, had eventually disappeared from her life when Terri's parents realized how dangerous it was for two teenage girls trying to flee tabloid reporters on their own.

Regina understood—especially after the late-night car wreck while trying to shake the paparazzi had almost killed her during her undergraduate years. But understanding why her friends had vanished didn't make those years any less painful. She nibbled a square of smoked gouda and hoped she could change the subject soon.

"Well, I'm glad our paths crossed," Devon said, lifting his glass. "Here's to finding new friends in unexpected places."

She felt her chest constrict, hating the lies but knowing she had no choice if she wanted to discover the truth about his father's finances.

"To new friends." Raising her glass, she clinked it gently against his.

Their eyes met as they drank. She glanced away fast, but not before she felt an undeniable spark between them. The thought he'd put into the meal, the curiosity he'd shown about her personally, the way he looked at her—all of it added up to frank male interest that would have been flattering if it hadn't been so dangerous to her mission.

"What about you?" She reached for another topic of conversation to steer things away from herself. Away from the slow simmer of awareness in her veins. "Where's home for you?"

"New York. I bought a place on Central Park West when I heard about a potential vacancy and jumped on it before the apartment went on the market." Crunching into an apple slice, he pointed to a low-flying hawk circling nearby. "My family is in Connecticut. Except, of course, for Marcus out in Los Angeles."

She tracked the bird while she thought about how to steer the conversation to find out more about his father. The hawk flew for long moments without flapping its wings, angling through the air in a grace-ful, soaring flight.

"Do you travel to a lot of different places for work?" She needed to be subtler than she'd been earlier. She might have admitted she'd read up on his family, but she didn't want him to know how much.

"I was in India last week, meeting with an inter-national client, but that's rare." He removed a sheaf of paperwork from his jacket and laid it on the table. She recognized a map of Mesa Falls Ranch with a few of the buildings marked on it. "Montana is new for me, too, and I appreciate the tour today." He spun the map around so she could see it better, then pointed to a few pen markings. "I want to make sure we hit these places."

She recognized two of the owners' homes as well as a peak with renowned views of the valley. But her eye was drawn to the papers that had been behind the map—the ones now partially covered by his forearm. The top sheet appeared to be contact information for someone—part of a phone number and an email address that looked like it ended "...tigations.com."

Mitigations? Litigations? Investigations?

"Of course." Her brain worked double time to come up with other words even as she forced her-self to make eye contact with him. "No problem."

Crazy though it might seem, she couldn't shake the feeling the information was related to his fa-ther's estate. Or the book. Or something that might shed light on her quest. But how to steal a peek at it?

"Excellent." He started to slide the map back into

his stack, then paused. "Did you need this for reference?"

Her gaze flicked back to the sheaf on the table, where she caught the word "April." Or was it a name?

"Sure." She reached for the map, trying not to stare at the place where his elbow hid whatever came after "April."

"That would be great."

He hesitated before passing it to her. "Are you okay?"

She forced her attention back to his green eyes. "Of course. Why?"

Tucking the map into her jacket pocket, she watched him fold his documents and return them to his coat.

"You just seem a little distracted." He studied her, and for a moment she feared he could see right through her. But then he clinked his glass to hers again. "Drink up, Regina. We should probably pack our things so we have time to see the rest of the ranch."

Nodding, she finished her meal and wondered how to see those papers before they disappeared for good. One way or another, she needed a plan to separate Devon from his jacket as soon as possible.

Something seemed off about the lovely Mesa Falls Ranch trail guide.

Devon couldn't quite put his finger on what it was, though. After they returned their mounts to the stables shortly before sunset, Regina had invited him to brush down the horses with her, one of many little things that struck him as odd. He didn't mind taking care of an animal he'd ridden all day—that was far from the point. Mesa Falls Ranch was positioning itself as a high-end corporate retreat, secondary to its main ranching mission. They had plenty of ranch hands to oversee the stables. If anything, they had too much help in the weeks before the launch party. So certainly, Regina didn't need his help.

As much as he'd like to think the sexy trail guide was unwilling to part with his company, he didn't think attraction factored into her request. There'd been plenty of opportunities to act on the awareness between them today—during lunch especially. But Regina had seemed distracted, her thoughts elsewhere.

He ran the brush over Evangeline's flank, working in tandem with Regina in the quiet barn. The riding arena close to the lodge was more of a showplace than part of the working ranch—here, inexperienced riders could receive pointers about horsemanship, or try their hand at simple rodeo events in a well-monitored setting. Only a handful of horses were housed here tonight. The sweet smell of hay circulated in the cool air from a high, open window.

Evangeline whinnied as he moved the brush down her back, and he caught sight of Regina working silently at the crossties, next to him. Her dark hair caught the overhead lights, revealing a healthy shine. She'd shrugged off her jacket when they'd started working and now he did the same, draping it over the hook near hers. Even with the window open, the big animals warmed the space.

Regina caught him staring then, and for a moment the temperature spiked hotter. Her eyes darted over him before she shifted her attention back to her work. What was it about her silvery gaze that made him so damned curious about her? Maybe the odd signals he'd gotten today came down to attraction after all.

Perhaps she was simply shy. Or maybe she felt an abundance of caution since she was employed by the ranch and didn't wish to risk a new job by fraternizing with a client. While he considered his next move, his phone rang. He'd had it turned off during their ride, so he checked the screen now just in case it was important.

The caller ID showed his mother's photo.

"Regina, I just need five minutes, but I really should grab this."

"Of course." She waved him along, her smile transforming her face from pretty to breathtaking. "Take as long as you need."

Nodding his thanks, he set down the brush and hit the button to connect the call.

"Mom?" He moved toward the barn doors, sliding one open to step outside.

"Hello, Devon." Her voice was lowered, and he could hear what sounded like a dinner party in the background—indistinct music, soft chatter and laughter. "I just saw your note about extending your stay in Montana for the launch party. I wanted to be sure you'll be here for the wedding."

"Of course I will." He thought he'd made that clear in the text he'd sent earlier, but he knew his mother was nervous about her upcoming nuptials. "Mom, I wouldn't miss it for the world. You know that."

"Okay." Her small laugh sounded relieved more than anything. "I thought so, but I wanted to be sure. There's so much booked for the week before that the sooner you can be here the better."

Devon breathed in the deep stillness of the Montana mountains, wishing he could trade places with his mother for a few days so she could enjoy the peace of this kind of setting. Then again, she wouldn't want to travel anywhere that his father had frequented. She'd never forgiven him for not sticking around after Devon was born, and although Devon understood why, he wished—for her sake—she'd been able to put Alonzo firmly in her past a long time ago.

"I'll be at the rehearsal dinner." He glanced behind him at the barn door, which he'd left open a few inches. "Is there anything else going on that I should know about?"

He tried his damnedest to be an attentive son. His mother had never held it against him that he was a Salazar, the way Granddad did, even though Devon had worked hard to make sure he didn't overtly share any of his dad's qualities.

"Most of Bradley's family will be in town, so Granddad wants to roll out the red carpet," his mother explained. Bradley Stewart's family was a force to be reckoned with in banking, a well-connected clan Devon's grandfather would leverage at first opportunity. "There will be a welcome party, a few media interviews, that sort of thing. You're always so good with the press, Devon. I'd love it if you could be here."

He closed his eyes, resenting his grandfather for making this wedding about business. And he hated knowing that news of Alonzo Salazar's salacious book could steal the spotlight from what should be the happiest day of his mother's life.

"The launch party is only two days before the wedding." He couldn't leave before then. Still, guilt gnawed at him that he couldn't be there for her when she'd given up so much for him. "But I'll get a flight as soon as it ends."

"Of course. I understand." The music in the background of the call grew louder. "I'd better go now, darling. Good luck, and I'll see you soon."

He disconnected the call, not happy to disappoint her, but knowing that it was more important for her to have him here—though she'd never understand why.

Devon needed to speak to all the owners of Mesa Falls Ranch to see what they knew about his father's past—about the book, about the proceeds, about their relationship with him. But he needed to keep a lid on scandal at all costs. Keep his family's private business just that—private.

And yet, as he peered through the opening of the barn door, Devon spotted Regina Flores hunched over his discarded jacket, his personal papers spilled over her lap while she helped herself to the confidential contents.

Anger flared—fast and hot.

Shoving open the door the rest of the way, he charged toward her. Her guilty scramble to stash the papers would have been damning even if he hadn't already seen her reading them.

He stopped a foot away from her, quietly seething. "May I ask what in the hell you think you're doing?"

Three

Regina froze.

She'd thought she'd been keeping an ear out for Devon's return, but she'd gotten engrossed in reading the files she had only meant to photograph. Had he seen her with the papers? Or had he only noticed her rifling through his jacket?

Her heart pounded harder as she relinquished her hold on his coat, letting it fall back on the chair as she straightened.

"I'm so embarrassed." She only had so many ways to play this without alienating him. For that matter, if she didn't find a way to smooth this over, he could have her fired from her job and then she'd *really* have no options left to track down the profits from the book that had ruined her family.

"With good reason." Devon glared at her, his shoulders tight and his jaw clenched. He stalked closer, his dark brows furrowed.

Behind her, Evangeline tossed her head and exhaled on a long, shuddering snort. Regina moved away from the mare, not wanting the animals to feel the nervous energy pinging through her. Stepping from the straw-covered grooming area onto the cement walkway down the center of the barn, she kept her gaze trained on Devon.

"I only wanted to touch your jacket." She knew her cheeks were bright red, and in this case that was surely to her advantage. "I'm sure it's obvious to you that I'm..." She forced herself to pause, wishing there was another way out of this mess. She took a deep breath. "Attracted to you."

It wasn't a lie. She let him see the truth of it in her expression. Her pulse galloped faster while his green eyes narrowed.

"And what did you think you might find out by snooping around in my personal papers?"

Did he know that for certain? Or was he guessing?

"Call me crazy." Shrugging, she folded her arms around herself to ward off the chill of his doubt. "But I just wanted to breathe in the scent of you." That part was—sadly—true, as well. The first thing she'd done when she picked up his coat was to bury her nose in the lining. "And the papers fell out."

Her face must be on fire by now. She swore she

could feel where every single capillary pulsed with heat just below the skin.

She was worried about his reaction, yes. And she'd stretched the truth. But maybe the biggest reason for her blush was that she was baring a secret she hadn't wanted to admit—even to herself.

"I find that difficult to believe when you seemed careful to keep me at arm's length today." He spoke softly, studying her carefully as he stood just inches away. "Our picnic certainly offered an opportunity for that."

"Fraternizing with a guest will surely be frowned upon by my new employer." Her breath came fast. Out of the corner of her eye, she could see a stray hair flutter in her exhale. "I didn't think acting on the attraction would be wise." She saw some subtle shift in his expression. His pupils widened, maybe. Or his nostrils flared. "I still don't," she rushed to add.

"Nevertheless." He shifted closer, his right hand grazing her jaw to lift her chin. "I'd like to test the truth of that claim."

The green of his eyes was just the slimmest of rings around the dark centers as he peered down at her. Her thoughts scrambled.

"That I don't think we should act on it?" Her breathless voice sounded nothing like her.

"That you're attracted to me." His thumb skimmed along her lower lip and pleasure trembled through her even though she tried to hold herself very still.

Electrified, she sucked in a breath. And then his lips were brushing hers. Once. Twice. Just feather-soft touches that made her knees weak, right before he kissed her.

For real.

Desire streaked through her and stole her reservations. Her arms fell to her sides for only a moment before she wrapped them around him, drawing him closer. The woodsy bergamot scent of his skin filled her senses while his hands slid around her back, pressing her closer. His fingers flexed against the hem of her sweater, stirring an awareness of how much more pleasure awaited her. The hard wall of his chest called to her palms to explore all the intriguing ridges and planes of muscle...

He broke away suddenly. For a moment, she was utterly disoriented, blinking back at him in the glow of the barn light overhead. Her breath came hard, and she noticed his did, too. His hands lingered on her back, while hers still clutched the shoulders of his gray flannel shirt. With an effort, she unclenched her fingers, letting go of him.

"The chemistry is real enough." He didn't seem in any hurry to release her, his fingers skimming around to her waist. Stroking up her arms. "But is your story?"

His icy words jerked her back to reality.

He let go of her then, pacing away from her. For a moment she didn't even remember what he was talking about. She'd been that caught up in the kiss.

Panic lodged in her throat.

"What do you mean?" She stalled for time, not sure how to fix this.

How could she have let him catch her snooping? And why hadn't she used the time when they'd been kissing to work out a plan B? Absurdly, her lips still tingled from that damned kiss, and it was all she could do not to brush her fingers over her mouth to still the quivery feeling.

"I mean I'm not convinced about your motives." He turned to study her, and she wondered how he could flip the switch from passion to interrogation so fast. "You could be using the attraction as a smoke screen. A very hot, very effective smoke screen, from whatever it is you're up to."

Her throat dried up.

She was on the verge of blurting the truth—that she didn't trust him, either, and she wanted to know what his father had done with all the profits from her misery. But then, Devon took a step closer to her again, his head tilting to one side as if he was considering a new idea.

"Maybe the best solution is for me to keep you close so I can have my eyes on you all the time." His wolfish smile shouldn't have been a turn-on, but she'd be lying if she denied a flare of heat inside her.

"I don't understand," she told him flatly, folding her arms across her chest to quiet all the ridiculous reactions of her body.

"We'll act on the attraction, Regina," he announced, like it was already decided. "Explore this chemistry for as long as we have together." He lowered his voice, the silky tone stroking over her senses like a caress. "Starting now."

* * *

Checkmate.

He'd effectively cornered her, and he wondered if she'd give up the game. No more pretense.

Because while there was attraction at work here—without question—he felt like she'd been searching his jacket with a purpose. His every instinct screamed at him that she was looking for something specific. Was she with the press? Had someone in the media gotten wind of his father's secret identity?

Or had she been tasked by her employer to find out more about him before the launch party? Devon suspected the Mesa Falls Ranch owners would have preferred to work with Marcus on the launch since Devon had arrived late and had asked a private investigator to look into his father's doings before he'd arrived. Weston Rivera hadn't been pleased to be contacted by the PI.

Devon had hoped that was water under the bridge after the welcome reception the owners had thrown last week. But now he wasn't so sure.

"You're suggesting we…date?" When she raised one eyebrow and pursed her lips, there was something familiar about her features.

For a moment, he could almost swear he'd seen her before. But that made no sense. He shoved aside the thought to lock things down with her.

"Date. And wherever that might lead." He wandered closer to her again, taking pleasure in the way her gaze dipped to his lips for a moment.

"I have to admit, now I'm the one confused about

your motives." She turned to release her horse from the crossties so she could lead the bay back to a stall.

It forced Devon to back up a step. The scent of hay and horses stirred while the mustang swished her tail, settling into the space before dipping her muzzle into the feed bucket.

"I thought I made myself very clear. I'm attracted to you. The feeling is reciprocated." He shrugged as he moved toward Evangeline so he could put her in for the night, too. "What's confusing about that?"

"You don't seem to trust me." She eyed him warily, opening another stall door and showing him where to lead Evangeline. "That kiss felt like some kind of test. You walked away from it easily enough. And now you toss around the idea of dating like it's a dare."

"In a way, it is." He led Evangeline to the stall, then passed the bridle to Regina. "Do you dare?"

She slanted a sideways glance at him while she waited for Evangeline to get comfortable. Then she pulled off the bridle and latched the stall door.

"That's beside the point. I can't risk my job by dating one of the patrons." She brushed past him with two bridles in hand.

He followed her into the tack room, where the scent of leather cleaner and polish hung heavily in the air. The walls were lined with saddles, blankets and all kinds of riding accessories. There were a few highly decorative pieces, but most were well-used plain leather.

"I'm not a guest of the ranch, though," he reminded her as he watched her wipe down the bridles. "I'm a freelance contractor providing a service. That's something very different. No one will object to you seeing me for the next ten days until the launch party."

He needed to keep her close to him to find out what she was doing. If she was trying to dig up information about his family, he'd find out soon enough. He watched as she hung the clean bridles on an iron peg over her head. She arched up on her toes, fitting the pieces over the hook.

"How do I know that?" She lifted her hands in exasperation.

"I'll inform Rivera personally." He rested his hands on her shoulders, feeling the tension threaded through her muscles under the fabric of her soft chambray shirt. "That way, he'll know I'm the one who initiated this relationship. So tell me, what would you like to do tomorrow to celebrate our first date?"

He caught a hint of her fragrance, something green and fresh like spring. Jasmine, maybe. He could feel some of the knots sliding away as he worked over the muscles. Not all. She was far from relaxed. Because she was nervous? Or was it more of that attraction at work? The kiss had rocked him, too, even if he'd managed to hide his reaction better than she had.

"You're serious about going through with this?" Those silver eyes were so wary.

"I want you," he told her simply. "I'm sure you could tell how much when I kissed you."

He saw a shiver pass over her and it filled him with satisfaction. No matter what other dynamic was at work between them, he couldn't wait to touch her again. Taste her thoroughly.

She gave a quick, fast nod.

"Okay."

It wasn't the most enthusiastic of receptions, but the shiver—and the kiss—had been enough.

"Okay." He confirmed it, gesturing her to lead the way out of the tack room.

She sidled past him, careful not to touch.

He retrieved her discarded jacket and helped her on with it. "Would you prefer I make the plans?"

He took his time easing the heavy duster over her shoulders, then lifted her hair out from under the collar. It brushed in a silky waterfall along the top of her back.

"Maybe that would be best." She turned to face him while he shrugged into his own jacket. "The picnic was nice today," she admitted, a smile animating her features for the briefest moment.

"I'm glad you had fun." He looked forward to getting to know Regina Flores much, much better. "I'll find a way to top it tomorrow."

She tugged her gloves from her pockets and pulled them on, flexing her fingers into the leather. He wondered what she was thinking. Feeling.

There were mysteries in her eyes he couldn't wait to unravel.

"I'll pick you up at six?" He pulled open the barn door so he could walk her back to her cabin or wherever it was she stayed on the ranch.

Snowflakes still fell in slow whorls. She glanced up at the sky and then back at him as she stepped outside.

He couldn't miss the steely gleam in her eyes when she nodded.

"I'll be ready." Bracing her shoulders, she headed into the wind.

Devon followed and escorted her toward the main lodge. He'd have time to do his homework on Regina tonight, even if that meant asking his private investigator to do some digging on her. And when it was time for his date with the mysterious trail guide?

He'd be ready, too.

She was dating the enemy.

An hour after she'd made the deal with Devon, Regina couldn't decide if she was grateful for her quick thinking that had made her tell him she was attracted to him. Because she sure had put herself between a rock and a…very hard place. Memories of that kiss still scorched her insides if she let her thoughts linger on it too long.

Back in the comfort of her own quarters that night, she tried to focus on what she'd learned from her gamble instead of the dicey situation she'd put herself in. With a pillow propped behind her back as she worked in bed, she recorded everything she remembered from her quick glance through Devon's papers, entering the information on her laptop.

The women's bunkhouse accommodations were snug but comfortable, especially since half of the beds were still vacant. But then, the guest ranch portion of Mesa Falls was all new, with the service positions still being filled. She'd chosen a top bunk in the corner, and between the location and the curtains she could draw closed across the open side of the bed, her work on the laptop was private enough.

One of the other women she roomed with had come in briefly to shower before heading out for the night, and another had gone to sleep early. In the common room where there were a few couches and a television, a couple of older ladies who worked in the kitchens were reading. Someone had flipped on Christmas country tunes in that room, the occasional twang of a fiddle or a steel guitar filtering back to the bunk area. Regina didn't think anyone would disturb her for the rest of the evening with her curtain closed. She had her phone charging next to a bottle of water in a canvas cupholder that dangled from the top rail against the wall.

Regina searched online for the name she recalled from Devon's papers: April Stephens. She was a private investigator. She hadn't recalled the contact information other than that the woman was based in Denver. Regina found her easily and read her bio on a website for an agency specializing in forensic accounting and tracking down hidden assets.

Why did Devon have her card? And whose assets did he need to trace? Delving further into the website, she found links to articles about tracking missing persons. Apparently the two investigative specialties often went hand in hand since tracing missing money often led to missing people.

For the first time, Regina felt a twinge of guilt about invading Devon's privacy. She'd been so convinced he was profiting from the story about her family, but what if he wasn't? What if she was being as careless sifting through his personal business as his father had been with her family's secrets?

The scent of popcorn from the common room pulled her out of her thoughts, making her remember she hadn't eaten since the picnic she'd shared with Devon. Her stomach rumbled.

The other papers she'd glimpsed in Devon's coat were return plane tickets and a printed schedule for an East Coast wedding. A quick scan online confirmed the woman getting married was Devon's mother, Katherine "Kate" Radcliffe. Regina had read about Kate briefly in her earlier investigation into the Salazar family, but since the woman had never been a Salazar and didn't stay with Alonzo for long, Regina hadn't devoted much time to learning about the Radcliffes.

She dug deeper now, clicking through article after article online to discover all she could about Philip Radcliffe, the aging patriarch who oversaw a global pharmaceutical company. It was possible his wealth had helped Devon fund Salazar Media, and not Alonzo Salazar's ill-gotten gains. But an interview with the billionaire in a business publication suggested otherwise. In it, Philip talked about the need for "the Radcliffe fortune to remain in Radcliffe hands" for future generations.

That sounded like a deliberate slight to his grandson with a different last name, and the author of the article had speculated as much.

Fingers hovering over her keyboard, Regina found herself empathizing—at least a small amount—with Devon. She recalled how it felt to be dismissed based on lack of birthright.

While she mulled over the new twists, the sound of footsteps in the bunkhouse made her click off her screen right before a shadow loomed on the drawn curtain around her bed.

"Hon, you still awake?" It was a woman's voice, warm and kind.

Regina pushed aside the lined cotton fabric to see Millie, one of the new line cooks, holding a bowl of popcorn. Millie seemed close to retirement age, but she had an energetic vibe and fully embraced ranch life. Her long blond braid rested on the shoulder of a red thermal shirt that read Santa, I Tried.

"Just doing some research before bed," Regina replied, pointing to the closed laptop.

"We made a second batch of popcorn, so I thought I'd see if you wanted a bowl." Millie winked as she extended a red plastic dish decorated with green horseshoes and Christmas trees, with a paper napkin underneath. "It's got extra butter."

Touched by the gesture, Regina smiled, her mouth

watering. "That's so kind of you to think of me. Thank you."

"It's no trouble." Millie was already backing away, her voice quiet as she passed another bunk where one of the room attendants was sacked out cold.

Millie disappeared into the common room, leaving Regina with the popcorn and a surprise dose of holiday spirit she hadn't been expecting. It was strange that she felt sort of at home at Mesa Falls Ranch, given that she'd only come here to learn more about the Salazar heirs. But it had been a long time since she'd been able to work with horses; the man she'd thought was her father had confiscated her beloved Arabian when the book scandal broke. She'd missed that equine companionship almost as much as she'd missed her father figure. More, perhaps, since the horse hadn't discarded her the way her dad had.

Mesa Falls Ranch gave her the gift of horses. And, it seemed, the gift of friendly faces in the form of people like Millie. As Regina munched the popcorn, she reminded herself not to get too attached. Because she was only in Montana for one reason.

To find out where Alonzo Salazar's profits went on the book that stole Regina's life out from under her. And to do that, she was going to get closer to Alonzo's oldest son than she'd ever imagined.

Starting tomorrow, on whatever date Devon dreamed up for them.

She wished she could concentrate on how that would benefit her cause. Yet long after she'd finished the popcorn and tried to fall asleep, Regina's thoughts returned again and again to the spark of awareness she'd felt when Devon had kissed her. And the knowledge that she was getting in too deep with a man who compelled her like no other.

Four

April Stephens tipped her face into the wind off the Bitterroot Mountains, breathing in the freedom of Big Sky Country just before sunset on her first day in Montana.

Gripping the smooth trunk of a sapling close to the campsite she'd just finished securing, April took in the beauty of Gem Lake, a frozen patch of opalescent blue in the gully between sharp gray peaks. Her work as a private investigator for Devon Salazar may have paid for her plane ticket, but that didn't mean her new client owned all of her time. As soon as she'd settled her things in her room at the Great Lodge at Mesa Falls Ranch, April had stuffed her camping gear into a backpack and requested a ranch utility vehicle to take her to one of the trailheads for Trapper's Peak.

She had no need to summit, and there wouldn't have been enough time if she'd wanted to. She just needed this moment in the outdoors with space and air around her, so different from the crammed suffocation of her mother's house, full of things from years of hoarding, every precarious pile providing tangible evidence that April could never save her.

Her trip there this morning, before her flight to Montana, had been a typical exercise in futility. She'd wanted to bring her mom some basic groceries, encourage her to get in the shower and alert her that April was going out of town. Instead, Mom had spent the whole time fretting over where to put a recent purchase of fabric remains from a local shop going out of business. By the time April had left for the airport, her mother—once a beloved schoolteacher and warm-hearted homemaker—had been in tears trying to cram bolts of fabric around the refrigerator in a way that would still allow the fridge to open.

Shoving aside the memory, April breathed deep, savoring the clean air before turning back to her camp and the small fire she'd started. She took a seat in front of the blaze to enjoy the warmth for another hour until she crawled inside her small tent for the night. She needed to be ready to break camp at dawn and get back to the lodge. For now, however, the cold wind tore through her clothes, whipping them against her in a way that felt like Mother Nature shaking out the cobwebs. Snow swirled in white eddies, the damp iciness scrubbing away the detritus of the messy life she kept hidden from everyone.

Was it any wonder she enjoyed tracking down secrets? She spent so much time concealing her own it was a weird sort of therapy to rip away the subterfuge from other people's. Sometimes it felt cruel. But it was cathartic, too.

Like with her work for Devon Salazar, who now wanted answers about Regina Flores on top of his original request. Tomorrow, she would meet with him about his more difficult project—tracking the proceeds from his father's book. But tonight, before his date with the mysterious Regina, she'd had to message him a warning that the woman's identity was an obvious fake.

That facet of the job had been easy—she'd been able to do the search on the flight. Without further information, she couldn't pinpoint the woman's real name. But as for the lady she claimed to be?

Regina Flores simply didn't exist.

The bunkhouse bustled with activity late the next afternoon while Regina dressed for her date. The second-shift workers had already left, and several of the women who held first-shift jobs were also getting ready to go out to local pubs, enjoying the start of the weekend.

Christmas pop music played over someone's speaker while women traded news about the workday. Most of the chatter was about the influx of reservations for the launch party week. Apparently, the lodge was already booked to capacity for the four days leading up to the event, and even now they were near 80 percent.

After pulling a heavy fisherman's sweater over her T-shirt, Regina double-checked an earlier text she'd received from Devon asking her to dress warmly since their date would have them outdoors for an hour. She was curious what he had in mind since the sun went down early this time of year. It was dark outside already.

She grabbed a pair of mittens and her jacket and was heading for the door when a snippet of conversation from the common room caught her ear.

"…I think his name is Devon. And he's smoking hot," a feminine voice spoke in a breathless rush, bringing Regina to an abrupt halt. "He came into the lodge today to make a reservation and I was so tongue-tied I don't even remember what he said to me."

Regina couldn't help but listen. But the response of the woman's friend was lost to Regina's ears when someone flipped on a hair dryer nearby. Of course, she shouldn't be eavesdropping anyhow, but it seemed reassuring to know she wasn't the only one who found the marketing executive from New York to be ridiculously appealing. Clearly, he affected total strangers that way, too.

Charging into the common room, she gave a wave to the three younger women decorating a small Christmas tree someone had put up in a corner. There were popcorn strands all around it. Regina guessed that was what Millie and her friends had been work-ing on the night before. Now the younger group—all from guest services, she thought—were hanging pine cones and small, glittery stars on the tree.

"Have a good night," one of them called to her as she left for her date.

She hadn't even pulled the door closed behind her when she spotted the sleigh.

The huge wooden contraption rested across the walkway in front of the bunkhouse. It was outlined in white lights and decorated with pine branches and a few red bows. A driver in a parka and Stetson held the reins to matching Friesian horses stamping and snorting in the chilly evening.

Devon stood beside the sleigh in a dark overcoat, jeans and boots, with a bouquet of white poinsettias in one hand.

Behind her, Regina felt her fellow bunkmates jos-tle for position to see. One woman let out a dreamy sigh while another squealed. Reactions Regina could completely understand.

But she knew this romantic display wasn't so much for her as a way for Devon to keep close to her. He was as suspicious of her as she was of him, and she couldn't allow herself to forget it.

"Are you ready for a sleigh ride?" he asked, strid-ing toward her.

She met him halfway, bearing in mind the cha-rade was temporary and strictly for the convenience of keeping an eye on her, so there was no reason to feel flattered he'd gone to this much trouble for their evening together.

"Very ready." As her boots crunched in the snow, her gaze fixed on her companion for the evening.

His green eyes held hers, his shadowed jaw calling to her fingertips to test the feel of his skin there.

"For you." His breath huffed in the air between them as he handed her the poinsettia bouquet tied with a red bow. The scent of his aftershave, something woodsy with a hint of spice, made her want to lean closer.

"Thank you." She clutched the cloth bow and inhaled the bouquet made fragrant by the balsam greenery around it. "They're beautiful."

"Good." He nodded his satisfaction, his breath puffing in the space between them. "I hope it's one of many things you enjoy about the evening." His hand landed on her back as he guided her toward the sleigh. "I've heard this tour is fun at night even though you aren't able to see the sights, as well."

Stepping up into the vehicle, she said hello to the driver before taking a seat on the bench padded with blankets in back. She'd worn a short wool jacket over her sweater, but there was a stack of extra quilts neatly folded in an open shelf under the front seat.

Regina set the flowers on one side of her while Devon settled into the spot on her other side. She could see her bunkmates still crowded in the front door, peering out at them. Their relationship had gone public in a hurry. No doubt it all looked wildly romantic to an outsider. Who would ever guess at the strange way she'd fallen into this evening with Devon?

"Did you speak to Mr. Rivera about...us?" She didn't want to give her boss any reason to fire her.

"I did." He nodded as he leaned back in the seat, draping one arm across the back of the bench behind her before giving the driver the cue they were ready. "And it's a nonissue as far as the ranch is concerned. He said they welcome a lot of couples who take temporary jobs together to experience ranch life."

The sleigh ride began while Regina digested the news, realizing there would be no getting out of the date for that reason. For better or worse, she was committed to this fake relationship if she wanted to learn more about Devon. But she planned to proceed with caution since she had the feeling Devon Salazar was a man who wouldn't take kindly to being deceived.

"I appreciate you checking with him," she told him sincerely, figuring if she spoke the truth as often as possible, it would go a long way to putting them both more at ease.

She glanced out over the moonlit snow as the horses trotted away from the ranch buildings on the trail connecting grazing pastures. The lane was well packed here because trucks and ranch utility vehicles used it frequently. The sleigh moved faster, the runners making a gentle swishing sound.

The evening was clear and starlit, but now and then she felt the kiss of snow against her cheeks from drifts blowing along either side of the trail.

"I'm glad I could put your mind at ease," Devon assured her, tipping his head back to stare up at the tree branches when they entered a heavily forested area next to a pasture. "Now that there's no reason to fear repercussions for you at work, we can relax and get to know each other better."

He turned toward her, his presence suddenly very near. Close enough for her to feel the warmth of his chest near hers, the brush of his arm against the back of her shoulders. His leg grazed hers. Her throat dried up at the physical proximity, at the appeal of hard male muscle just underneath a layer of clothes.

She hid a shiver that was more pleasure than worry.

Frowning, he leaned forward to retrieve one of the linens folded beneath the vacant seat in front of them.

"Are you cold?" he asked, already unfurling the red plaid wool and laying it over their laps. "There are plenty of blankets if you want another."

His fingers tugged the fabric around her, tucking it behind her hip, igniting a slow burn of awareness in her belly. And lower.

"I'm fine," she protested, mostly because his hands were a major distraction.

Her breath came faster as they emerged from the trees back out onto an open field, where it was brighter.

"Are you sure?" He studied her in the moonlight. "Just say the word if you want to turn back at any time." His concern sounded genuine.

"I'm warm enough." She fought the urge to lick

her dry lips—and battled an even stronger urge to taste her way along his shadowed jaw. She dragged her gaze from him to gesture toward the scenery. "And this is really pretty."

The Montana countryside unfolded in shades of gray and white around them as they skirted the western bank of the Bitterroot River. In the river valley, the waterway was a frozen layer of ice under snow, the area around it devoid of trees.

A few deer lifted their heads as the sleigh neared, keeping watch over Regina and Devon while other members of the herd nosed through the snow for a drink.

"We lucked out with the moon almost full." Devon shifted on the bench seat beside her as the sleigh took a hard turn away from the water. "I'd heard that the sleigh rides are worth it even when it's fully dark because of the sensory experience, but we're getting to see quite a bit, too."

"Sensory experience?" She wasn't quite sure what he meant. She pulled back to look at him.

"You know how your senses are heightened when your eyes are closed? You're more attuned to what you hear or feel? I heard this trip in the dark is fun like that—you can really enjoy the experience of the sleigh ride." A wolfish smile flashed as he lowered his voice. "Sort of like closing your eyes when you kiss so you can appreciate everything else that's going on."

Her belly flipped, feeling almost airborne for a moment.

Her brain refused to think of a single response that didn't sound like flirting. Because suddenly, all she could think about was pressing her lips to his.

Maybe it was unwise to kiss a woman who was hiding something from him.

Everything about Regina Flores—from her fake name to the way she'd rifled through his jacket the night before—had warned Devon she was trouble. At the very least, she was being dishonest with him.

Yet something about her called to him anyway.

Because he wasn't thinking about kissing the woman who was doing her best to deceive him. No, he was mesmerized by the one who could handle a horse in icy trail conditions and build her own fire. Captivated by the woman who knew about Montana wildlife and whose breath caught when he got close to her.

Like now.

"Should we try it?" he asked her now, skimming away a few dark strands of her hair where they blew across her cheek.

Her ivory-colored knit hat framed her face but didn't constrain her hair.

"Try what?" Her voice was a barely-there whisper of sound that was almost lost in the swish of the runners through the snow, the clop of hooves and the jangle of sleigh bells.

Regina's gray eyes were wide.

"The full sensory experience," he clarified, unable to move his fingers away from her face now that he'd felt the smooth softness of her skin. "The kiss."

Her nod was almost imperceptible. But she let her eyes drift closed, the dark lashes fanning a sultry shadow on her cheek.

Hunger for her surged. He wrapped his arm around her shoulders to draw her close and tipped her chin up to taste her the way he'd wanted to since the first time he'd seen her.

Her lips parted. He breathed in the minty trace of toothpaste and a fruity hint of lip balm before he kissed her. Gently, at first. Her mouth molded to his, lips pillow soft as she sighed into him.

Her fingers traced over his jaw, back and forth, before her hand fell to the shoulder of his jacket where she gripped the fabric tight. She edged closer, the warm press of her curves against him a welcome weight that took the kiss from experimental to simmering.

Awareness flared hotter, and he angled her shoulders to deepen the kiss. The small, needy sound she made at the back of her throat was like a torch to dry timber, desire for her cranking into a slow burn. Devon knew that a sleigh in the middle of a snow-covered Montana river valley was no place to take things farther. Yet that didn't do a damned thing to impede the roll of red-hot thoughts through his mind, the need for her scorching away everything else.

Especially when she fitted so perfectly against him under the cocoon of the wool blanket. Hip to hip. Thigh to thigh. And before he allowed his thoughts to drift any more astray, he forced himself to break the kiss. Slowly he leaned back, inserting an inch or two of space between them where before there'd been none.

The cold December air rushed in, filling the gap. Reminding him how much he needed things to cool down.

"I see what you mean now about the dark heightening the senses," Regina told him as she opened her eyes, her gaze seeking his. "I'm in complete, one-hundred-percent agreement that it's a very real phenomenon."

Devon breathed in the snow-dusted air as the sleigh bounced over frozen ruts in the ranch trail, the big black draft horses never slowing. Long, spikey shadows of pine trees fell over them. He waited for his heart rate to even out after the head rush of kissing Regina.

"I honestly didn't expect to prove the point so thoroughly." He'd planned to woo her into letting her guard down. Letting him see a glimpse of what she was really about. He hadn't expected to be seduced by a kiss. "It was my intention to take you out and get to know you better."

Hell, it had been his plan to confront her about her real motives. Her real identity. Running a social media company had taught him that people in her age demographic rarely if ever left no trace online. Yet that was the case with Regina Flores. The text message from his private investigator had confirmed his hunch—Regina was a fake.

"You asked all the questions at our picnic," she hedged, her fingers threading through the fringed edge of the blanket. "It's me who doesn't know much about you."

"I'm an open book," he protested, not surprised that she wanted to sidestep talking about herself. Maybe he'd do better to share something superficial about his world, in the hope that it would prompt her to share something, too. Like why had she taken the job at Mesa Falls Ranch. And why she was interested in him. "What do you want to know? And would you like some hot cocoa?"

He reached under the seat and retrieved two thermal carafes, passing one to her. He used the time to think through topics he needed to avoid if it turned out Regina was a member of the media looking for a scoop about his father's book.

And, hell, if the conversation got too dicey, he could always kiss her again. The chemistry between them was hot enough to burn away everything else.

"Thank you." She twisted the lid of her thermos to reveal the spout, and steam wafted out the top. "One thing I'm curious about is your job. Why did you start a media company?"

He seized on the topic to keep his thoughts from straying down the carnal path again. At least for the time being. Once they returned to civilization— maybe to the privacy of his cabin—he would be more than happy to revisit the temptation of Regina's lips.

"My brother, Marcus, has a gift for social media and a lot of ambition." Devon remembered seeing the kinds of things his brother posted in the early days of social media—innovative, creative content that people copied. "We've never had much in common, but I've always respected his intelligence. I had a strong feeling he would be successful, and I wanted to test my own ideas for growing a small business from the ground up."

Regina studied him for a long moment over the stainless steel rim of her drink. "Is it expensive to start a business like that? You must have been young."

"We both were. But there wasn't a lot of overhead at first—just the cost of manpower." He decided to mention his dad, if only to watch her reaction. "Our father invested in us, which helped."

Her head tilted a fraction at the mention of Alonzo. Was it polite curiosity? Or had she been waiting for a chance to discuss the author of the novel that had caused such scandal? He couldn't be sure.

"Nice to have a parent's support." She sipped her cocoa before continuing. "Is your dad an entrepreneur, too?"

"He was an English teacher, actually." He noticed how she peered down as he spoke, making it harder to gauge her reactions. "He died early this year."

"I'm so sorry." Regina's hand covered his, her tone undeniably sympathetic.

"Thank you." He missed his dad even though they'd never been close. If anything, that made it harder since he'd never have the chance to build a relationship with him now. "He taught at a boarding school on the West Coast. The same school the owners of Mesa Falls Ranch attended, in fact. My father remained in contact with them after graduation, visiting Montana whenever he had the chance."

He wondered about that. What had tied his father to the wealthy and powerful men who ran Mesa Falls Ranch? A small part of him resented the fact that his dad made time to see them, yet had rarely made the effort to spend time with Devon.

"No wonder the owners chose your firm to handle their social media as they open the ranch to private guests." She twisted the top closed on her drink and tucked the carafe into an open slot alongside the bench seat. "I'm sure it would make your father proud to know you and your brother are maintaining relationships that must have been important to him."

She sounded almost wistful as she said it, which made him wonder about her family.

"You said your mother lived in Tahoe," he said, recalling their conversation during the snowy picnic. "What about your dad?"

"We…aren't close," she admitted. "He was married to someone else when he had an affair with my mom, so I think I'm a reminder of his bad choices. Especially for my stepmother."

Before he could respond, she pointed into the field on their right. There, seemingly in the middle of nowhere, someone had decorated a pine tree with red and white lights. The blowing snow dulled some of them on the windward side, but the rest shone brightly.

"Are we close to one of the owners' homes?" he asked, trying to orient himself.

All six owners of the Mesa Falls Ranch had houses around the property. They'd seen a few of them on their horseback ride the day before.

She peered around the field, looking from the shadowed mountains to the river and back again. "Maybe Desmond Pierce's, although I don't think he's in Montana this week. And I don't see lights for a house anywhere nearby." She turned her gaze back toward him. "Although I've heard all the owners will be on hand for the launch event. How are the preparations going for that?"

Devon noted that she'd once again dodged the subject of her own life.

But now that she had nowhere to hide from his questions, he prepared to confront her with the bombshell that his investigator had shared with him.

"The preparations are running like clockwork. My biggest concern right now is you."

"Me?" She tilted her head, her expression questioning, but he didn't miss the hint of wariness in her eyes.

He met her gaze, the soft glow from the white lights on the sleigh helping him to see her even in the dark. "I can't figure out why you're hiding behind a fake identity."

Five

Panic bubbled up in her throat.

Not that she feared for her physical safety out here in the Montana wilderness, tucked into the back of the huge horse-drawn sleigh. Devon Salazar wasn't the kind of man to intimidate a woman; his demeanor was calm, his body language relaxed as he sat on the bench beside her. Plus, the sleigh driver from the ranch was right there, sitting high on his perch above the horses, a neutral party under his earmuffs and cowboy hat. He was far enough away from them not to hear their conversation, but close enough to remind Regina she wasn't alone with Devon.

So while she was safe, she was also well and truly cornered. There was zero doubt in Devon's eyes as he watched her every reaction to his accusation. And who knew how much she'd already given away in her shock? Her best option now was to tell him the truth.

Or at least enough truth to ease his suspicions.

"I have an excellent reason for hiding behind a fake identity." She retrieved the carafe of hot chocolate again, if only to soothe her dry throat—and to give her time to think her way through this. "I'm surprised you haven't guessed."

She twisted open the top and sipped the cocoa while the sleigh looped around an open field and turned back toward the ranch. A thin veil of snow kissed her cheeks as a cross breeze caught the flakes stirred by the runners. She welcomed the cooling touch against the knot of confusing emotions she had about this man. Resentment, anxiety and, yes, more than a little desire. She wished she didn't feel quite so much of the latter for a man whose father had been her worst enemy.

"I have ideas, certainly," he acknowledged as calmly as if they were discussing holiday decorations instead of her most closely guarded secrets. "And since you rifled through the papers in my jacket last night, you must know that I'm working with a private investigator, so I'll uncover the whole story for myself eventually." His level gaze revealed nothing. "But considering the draw between you and me, I'd prefer to hear the truth from you first."

Her stomach tightened. She could deny the sexual chemistry all she wanted, but at least he sensed it as much as she did. Why did she have to feel this

way about the man she was spying on? Her relationships before now had been predicated on mutual interests. They'd been simple, sensible connections.
They hadn't lasted long, but then again, they never
stirred this level of heat and confusion.

Steeling herself for the conversation, she lowered
her drink and closed the top again. "I couldn't risk
having you shut me out if you knew my real name,"
she admitted. "But I needed to meet you in person."

"Why?" he pressed. "What do you want from me?"

So many things now that she'd met him. She
wanted his touch. His kiss. His eyes on her because
he wanted her, not out of suspicion. But she was
foolish to think about that when there was something so much more complex between them. Something painful.

"I want answers about your father, Devon. About
the book he wrote that destroyed my life."

For a moment the only sound was the rhythmic
clomp of the horses' hooves, the soft rattle of their
dress tack against their bodies and the swish of the
runners through powdery snow.

In the quiet, Devon looked at her with the same
stunned expression that she suspected she'd worn
just moments before.

"*Your* life?" He leaned forward, his knee brushing hers, the warmth of his body stirring her in spite
of everything. "Who are you really?"

She wondered how he would react. Would he have
her fired? Or would he leave Mesa Falls Ranch alto-

gether and find someone else to oversee the launch event for his powerful client?

Those questions didn't begin to address the other fears and insecurities that came with revealing her identity. How many times had she been rejected because of her surname? Or turned into an object of scandal, ridicule or curiosity?

"I was born Georgiana. My original birth certificate had my name as Georgiana Cameron." She notched her chin higher, defensive of the girl she'd once been. "But in some ways, that name is far more deceptive than the one I'm using now."

Recognition flicked in his eyes. Something else flitted through his expression, too. Something dangerously close to pity.

"You're the daughter in that book?" He shook his head, eyes wide. "She was little more than a child—"

"I was sixteen when your father's book was released—almost seventeen by the time it was exposed that my parents were the key figures the novel was based on. And your father used a fake identity, too, I might add, for far more nefarious purposes than me. I need the anonymity to protect myself from the tabloids' relentless interest in me. But your dad? He used a pen name to hide behind. Plain and simple." She didn't have a prayer of disguising the bitterness in her voice. "I was twenty-one when I hired someone to investigate the pseudonym A. J. Sorensen, and it took two years to learn it was Alonzo Salazar."

"At which point, you learned he'd died." Devon put the pieces together quickly, but then, he was a sharp man to have taken his company from a start-up founded by two brothers to a globally recognized firm. "But why do you say your birth name is more deceptive than the one you're using now?"

The question tore at an old wound, one that had never healed. The anger it raised was never far from the surface, even in this beautiful, still Montana night.

"Because while I was born Georgiana Cameron, it was based on a lie." That was her mother's fault more than his father's. But there was plenty of blame to go around. "Have you read the book?"

A gust of wind whirled off the mountains and lifted the edge of the blanket, causing the fringe to dance across her lap.

"No." Devon smoothed the wool back into place as he shook his head. "I read a few reviews of it to get up to speed once I discovered Dad's...connection. So I know the gist, but not all the particulars."

"Lucky you," she said tightly, her fingers fisting in her gloves. "In a nutshell, the book depicts a sordid love triangle between a powerful Hollywood producer, an LA singer and a Brazilian soccer star, where the singer passes off her lover's child as her husband's." How many breathless reviews had she read that said the world it painted was so vivid and real, capturing the seedy side of fame? Tension knotted her shoulders. "But a few details were so par-ticular—like the singer being twice divorced and signing an ironclad prenup that gave her nothing if she cheated—that eventually a gossip columnist connected it to my parents. They were Hollywood actors and my mother's lover was an Argentinian polo player, but everything else lined up."

Her parents had met while her mother was in South America for her honeymoon, of all things, which was a tidbit of truth Regina wished she'd never learned. She'd loved the man she'd believed to be her father.

"It seems like a flimsy parallel—" Devon began, his expression thoughtful as the sleigh bumped from a field onto a path near the tree line.

His easy dismissal of that time in her life stirred a fresh wave of hurt.

"It became a national pastime to find other connections over the next six months. One of the tabloids offered a game with a huge cash prize for whoever found the most real-life similarities." It hadn't mattered for her by then, since her father believed the scandalmongers instantly. Her gut knotted. "But the most telling proof was the way my father—the man I'd believed to be my dad up until then—began divorce proceedings as soon as the story broke. I came home from dance practice one day to find a locksmith at work on the security system to ensure my mother and I weren't allowed back on his property."

She shouldn't feel tears burn at the back of her eyes about that anymore. But she rarely spoke about that day, and, yes, it still hurt.

Beside her, she heard Devon shift closer, his voice gentler. Kind.

"I'm sorry you had to endure that." He placed a

steadying hand between her shoulders. "And sorry that you weren't ever able to confront my dad about his actions. Hell, I wish *I* could ask him why he wrote that damned book, and I've only known about it for a few days. I can't imagine how deeply it's hurt you to have no answers."

His empathy touched her, even though she told herself she shouldn't let it. Because she couldn't afford to lose focus on her mission in Montana—to find out where the proceeds from the book had gone. And taking comfort from Devon's kindness would only make her feel worse later if she discovered his business was built on the income from her heartache.

"Thank you for your sympathy." She gave a clipped nod to acknowledge words that didn't heal the hurt of having her past ripped away. "And to your original point about Georgiana Cameron, my mother's husband won a court order to change my birth certificate so that it no longer bore his name."

There'd been a time when she'd had grand visions for what she would say to the man who'd raised her when she saw him in court—for the impassioned plea she would make about how a family wasn't bound by blood ties but by love. In her girlish dreams, she'd thought that could change his mind and make him accept her again. But he'd sent his attorney to argue for him, robbing her of the chance to gain closure by speaking directly to him.

"So Flores is your birth father's last name?" Devon asked.

"No. It's Fuentes. When I came up with a name

for myself, I used your father's trick of changing names just a little. In his book, my mother, Tabitha, was called Tempest. The man I believed to be my father, Davis, was called David." She shrugged, not owing him any more explanation than she'd already given. Yet now that she'd started talking about the past—about all the reasons she felt angry—she found it hard to stop. "Even as Georgiana Fuentes, the tabloids hounded me. It was so bad that I got into a car accident trying to elude a photographer. The surprise blessing of reconstructive surgery on my face was that at least I didn't bear as much resemblance to the woman I was before."

The surgeries had been painful. Recovery had been slow. But she'd used the time to formulate her plan for revenge. One that she couldn't abandon just because she was attracted to Alonzo Salazar's older son.

"Georgiana." He covered her hand with his where it rested on the blanket.

Even through her gloves she could feel the warmth of his palm. The sound of her name on his lips was oddly soothing. She hadn't heard it in so long. She'd isolated herself in so many ways, unhappy with the shreds of family she had left after the wreckage caused by that damned book.

"Please." Her throat burned with emotions as the sleigh hurtled faster toward the ranch. "Don't call me that."

She couldn't afford to let her feelings toward him soften. Part of her wanted to call an end to this conversation, but they were still too far from the ranch for her to get out and walk. She would have to sit tight, see how the conversation—and the attraction—played out.

"Regina, then," he corrected himself, the gentleness in his voice and his touch unnerving her. "I wish I could take back what he did. Or even help you to understand it, because I don't understand myself."

She willed herself to pull away from him but couldn't quite do it. Her emotions were ragged, and she feared one false move would dissolve all her boundaries and send her hurtling into his arms to seek what warmth she could in his embrace, to forget herself in the seductive power of his kiss.

She wanted the heat of their attraction to burn away everything else, if only for a few hours. And that was a dangerous desire when she should be focused on her end goal—finding out where the proceeds of that book had gone.

A goal she wasn't ready to admit to him. Because what if he thwarted her efforts to unravel the truth?

"So find the answers now," she challenged. "You said you hired a private investigator." She knew his budget would be far bigger than the measly amount she'd been able to pay someone to track the mystery author in the first place. "Why not ask the PI to find out your father's reasons for writing it?"

Devon studied the myriad emotions on Regina's face, visible even in the dim Christmas lights strewn around the outside of the sleigh. Her confession had rocked him, though he'd gone into the evening knowing that she wasn't who she claimed to be. Yet he hadn't expected anything like this—a revelation that she was a woman who'd been personally devastated by his father's book.

Even after all the ways she'd come clean tonight, Devon couldn't help the lingering sense that she'd held some piece back from him. Some part of the bigger picture he wasn't seeing yet.

Soon enough, he would. He just needed to bring himself up to speed on her and her family. Learn all he could about the Camerons, the Fuenteses, and about how his father's life had intersected with theirs. It seemed that the biggest mystery remained; Devon hadn't known his father at all.

For now, his need to stay close to Regina was stronger than ever. And not just because the air between them sizzled every time they looked at one another. But because he had to know what she was really up to in Montana this week. He didn't believe for a second that she'd come all this way, taking a job as a trail guide, just to learn more about his father's motives. Was she hoping to sue his family? Or look into his father's past for skeletons as some sort of payback scheme? She could certainly cause a scandal for him if she hoped to get even with the Salazars. There was more at play here, and Devon intended to uncover it.

More important, he planned to keep a lid on it until after his mother's wedding.

"Good idea about the investigator," he told her,

still holding her hand. Still wanting her in spite of everything. "I'll ask her to explore my father's past and see what she can come up with. I wasn't aware he had ties to the show business community, so I'm not sure where he would have unearthed information about your parents' private lives."

For that matter if Regina was considering a lawsuit against his father's estate, it might be beneficial to have the investigator's findings ready to shore up a defense. But Devon hoped it wouldn't come to that.

Regina slid her hand out of his and hugged herself. He mourned the loss of her touch.

"When I came to work here, I thought you might have those answers for me." Her restless gaze roamed the lights of the guest ranch buildings in the distance, momentarily visible from a high hill. "Knowing the author's reasons for exploiting my family might help me finally gain some closure, so I can put the past to rest for good."

Her words sparked a feeling of defensiveness for his dad, but not strongly enough to outweigh the empathy he felt for what she'd been through. Besides, whatever wrongs had been committed didn't detract from the simple fact that Devon wanted her with a hunger unlike anything he'd ever experienced.

"I wish I had answers, but all I have right now are more questions." He shifted closer to her, resting his fingertips lightly on her cheek to encourage her to meet his gaze. A thrill shot through him to touch her this way; her skin was cool and soft. "And right now the most important of those questions is this.

Will you have dinner with me?" he asked, looking deep into her gray eyes.

Her gaze lowered to his mouth and lingered.

"Dinner?" she asked after a long pause, pulling in a breath that huffed lightly along his palm.

Desire for her sharpened. Tightened. Crowded his chest.

"At my cabin," he clarified, wanting her to be very aware they would be alone. "I ordered catering for our return, but I don't want to be presumptuous. We can go out if you prefer."

Her tongue darted along her bottom lip.

"You still want this to be a date?" she asked, her voice wary. "Even now that you know who I am?"

"Knowing your identity doesn't change the attraction." If anything, the outing had only reinforced it. The memory of that kiss had never been far from his mind.

He stroked a light touch along her jaw, feathered a caress over her lush mouth.

Her eyelids fluttered but didn't close. "But my name…complicates things."

The sleigh skidded to the left down a hill and her body collided against his. He caught her, held her steady just long enough to feel the rapid-fire beat of her heart, the soft swell of her breasts. He wanted to feel her naked against him just this way.

He burned for her, his skin on fire. He breathed in the slightest hint of her jasmine fragrance, different from the cedar and balsam all around them.

"I think the rewards will make the complications

well worth it." It took a superhuman effort not to pull her closer. To slide his hands away. "But it's your call to make."

"You want me to decide." She worried her lower lip with her teeth in a movement as erotic as any touch.

He steeled himself, wondering how any woman could have this kind of power over him. Particularly a woman he shouldn't trust.

"I already know that I don't want tonight to end. But are you ready for more, Regina?" He kept his hands at his sides.

He knew his touch could sway her answer. That wasn't egotistical. It was a simple fact that they combusted when they touched each other.

And he refused to tip the scales unfairly. He needed her to be sure. To want this as much as he did.

The sleigh slowed down, and Devon knew they must be approaching the remote lodge where he was staying. The scent of wood smoke from a chimney fire teased his nose, reminding him he'd left a blaze burning in the river stone fireplace while the catering company set up service for the meal.

Fragrant cooking spices drifted on the breeze as the sleigh came to a stop. The driver remained in his seat, though he did turn around expectantly.

And still, Regina hadn't replied.

"Should we return to the ranch?" Devon didn't want to part company, but if that was her preference, he would wait.

Find a way to tempt her into another evening with him tomorrow.

"I don't run from complications, either," she finally said, certainty evident in every word as she peeled away the blanket and tossed it on the seat in front of them. Sitting forward, she gave him her hand. "And I signed up for a date tonight."

Six

Stepping over the threshold into the cabin perched above the Bitterroot River, Regina breathed in the savory scent of roasting spices along with the sweeter hints of nutmeg and clove. Devon took her coat from her before excusing himself to speak to the catering team.

In short order, the three staff members exited through a back entrance, leaving Devon and her very much alone. Warming trays filled the kitchen island, while the dining area table had been set with festive red candles and decorated with scattered pine cones on green boughs. The table was tucked into a nook of bay windows, but the sky remained too dark to see beyond the glass into the densely forested woods.

In the living area, a wood fire burned in the stone fireplace, casting an inviting glow over a deep leather sofa and a narrow holiday tree bare of all decoration except for white lights. The wide plank floors were covered with twill weavings in muted cream, gold and brown, in patterns she'd seen often in this part of Montana. Moose antlers hung over the fireplace.

Sliding off her boots, Regina left them by the front door and padded deeper into the lodge, pausing near the holiday tree. She tested the soft needles of the balsam pine, surprised to discover it was fresh.

A thrill shot through her as Devon's footsteps sounded behind her. She'd thought long and hard about his invitation here before setting foot inside. And now that she had made up her mind to be with him, she wasn't sure she could wait to kiss him again until after dinner.

"Regina." His voice was just over her shoulder.

His nearness made her heart gallop faster, the warmth of him close enough to make her nerve endings tingle with awareness. She was done questioning it. Done asking herself why she had to be so attracted to this man of all people.

The need for him was so strong she couldn't think past it.

She wasn't sure how to express any of that as she turned toward him. But when she met his gaze, she realized that she didn't need to try to articulate it. The sizzling connection sparked to life on its own, a magnetic draw so strong she couldn't say who moved first—him or her.

Their lips met. Fused. Arms wrapping around each other. Hers around his neck. His around her waist. The full-on impact of his body against hers was hot enough to take her breath away, stirring all her senses. She wanted time to appreciate every nuance of those sensations, and at the same time, she wanted more. Faster. Now.

His hands skimmed up her sweater, pressing her tighter. Her fingers raked through his wavy hair. The ripple of muscle under his shirt was enough to make her stomach tighten with breathless anticipation. Her pulse pounded harder in every tiny vein, making her whole body feel like a drumroll, a vibrating precursor to the big finish she craved.

When he broke the kiss, she made a sound of wordless protest, but then his lips fastened on her neck. She closed her eyes again to give herself to the feel of his tongue stroking along the exquisitely sensitive place behind her ear. Then the tender hollow at the base of her throat. Every sensual glide across her skin deepened the need to get closer. To be naked. To feel that good everywhere.

Tugging the hem of his shirt higher, she dragged it up and off. In the moment when his arms left her, she instinctively moved closer, craving his touch again. Her gaze fell to his broad chest, hands splaying over the bared skin. She would have kissed her way along one flat pectoral muscle, but with a low growl, he took her hand and drew her deeper into the cabin.

Following blindly—gladly—Regina passed the kitchen island into a darker hallway. Devon pushed open the door to the master suite. A desk lamp glowed on the far side of the king-size bed at the center of the room, the tan-and-gold-striped quilt half concealed by a rich red duvet folded at the foot of the mattress. She had a vague impression of high ceilings and dark wood beams, but then Devon's arms were around her again and she forget everything except for his touch.

His kiss.

Her lips found his with new urgency. The dance of his tongue along hers ignited a sensual shiver. Her hips arched against his. Seeking. Wanting.

His arms banded harder around her in answer, every inch of him steely and unyielding, making her melt. He stripped off her sweater and she shimmied out of her jeans, a new tension building inside her. She hadn't dressed for seduction, and for a split second, she wished she'd draped herself in sexy black silk instead of staid pink cotton.

Her gaze flicked up to his. He was taking her in with a frank male appreciation that sent any doubts fleeing. His focus narrowed to her breasts at the same time he slid aside the straps of her bra. Her breath caught as his eyes darkened, his fingers freeing the clasp just before his head lowered to capture a nipple between his lips.

A paroxysm of sensations coursed through her. Her head tipped back, and she gave herself up to the wicked skill of the kiss. He lifted her, depositing her gently onto the bed before his mouth moved to the other breast. She felt the delectable muscles of his shoulders and back flexing as he moved.

The ache between her thighs intensified. She lifted her hips, wriggling against him where his knee pressed into the bed. With a hungry groan, he lifted his head and shed his pants and his boxers. He retreated to the en suite bath for a moment and returned with a condom in hand, the packet already falling away in his rush to roll it into place. Heat and longing flooded her, her breathing fast and hard even though she'd done nothing more than kiss him. She thought she'd come right out of her skin if he didn't touch her soon.

Sitting up, she reached for him before he returned to the bed, her fingers trailing along the shadowed, incredibly sexy striations of his rigid abs. She didn't have long to admire him, though, because he slid his hands under her thighs before walking his fingers up her hips to draw down her panties.

The last garment between them finally removed.

He lifted her off the bed and she didn't hesitate to wrap her legs around him, her eyes on his. When he sat on the bed, she was on his lap. Straddling him. Trembling like it was her first time because the sensations were so intense.

She wrapped her arms around his neck, kissed him while he edged his way inside her. Joining them.

Pleasure crowded out everything else. Every touch, every taste, every stroke tantalized her, the passion building fast. She locked her heels behind him, holding him close while they moved in sync. Over and over.

Heat seared her. She closed her eyes again, wanting to focus on the sweetness of what he was doing to her. On his hands cupping her breasts, thumbs teasing over the peaks, his thighs flexing beneath her in a way that drove her right over the edge.

Her orgasm blindsided her, her feminine muscles seizing again and again, wringing out every shred of possible pleasure. She felt Devon go still beneath her for a moment before the same wave caught him, too, his body going rigid as his release pumped through him. It was impossibly good.

Pure and utter bliss.

And all she could do in the aftermath was tip her head to Devon's shoulder and cling to him because there were no words for what had just happened. Other people had sex. This?

She was pretty sure the earth had moved.

After long moments wrapped in each other's arms, he found a way to disentangle from her, pulling her back to lie beside him on the bed. He drew the spare blanket over their bodies while she tried to catch her breath.

Reason returned slowly, bringing with it new worries about what had just happened. As Devon smoothed back her hair, she was grateful for the long silence while she collected her thoughts. Tried to figure out what happened now.

Because no matter how good it had felt, Devon Salazar remained a potential enemy, as well as someone who had the answers to the puzzle of her shattered past. And she couldn't forget that, even for the sake of the best sex of her life.

"I can hear you thinking," he said finally, his voice a sexy whisper against her ear.

For a moment, she wished that this could be just a normal relationship where she could lean into him and savor what had just happened instead of thinking through her every move. But she hadn't come to Montana for romance. She needed to be careful around him, no matter how amazing he'd just made her feel.

While she debated her approach, Devon spoke again. "Before we try to figure out where things stand, why don't we put some clothes on and go have dinner?"

As he took another bite of a spiced scone with cinnamon glaze an hour later, Devon studied the woman across the table from him. She'd surprised him in so many ways tonight. First, when she'd come clean about her identity, it had rocked him. He'd imagined plenty of reasons for why she was pretending to be someone else, but it had never crossed his mind that Regina Flores had been born Georgiana Cameron, a woman caught in the crosshairs of the scandal created by his father's book.

Then, before he could wrap his head around what that meant, there'd been the unforgettable sex. Even now, after they'd enjoyed companionable conversation over roast duck, coconut-ginger yams and risotto with mushrooms, Devon's thoughts kept returning to what they'd shared. The connection had been unlike anything he'd ever known, scorching away the suspicions and deceits until there was nothing but burning need. And she had seemed as taken aback by their chemistry as he had been.

Now, after devouring the last of his dessert, he slid the dish aside and wondered how to proceed with the beautiful woman full of contradictions in front of him.

"More wine?" He lifted the bottle of port while Regina scooped up a forkful of gingerbread shortbread, one of three choices the caterers had left for them.

"No. Thank you." Her dark hair curled in waves around her face, the strands tousled from his fingers. "I have to be a trail guide early tomorrow morning."

She had put her jeans and sweater back on, and had the sleeves of the bulky knit pushed up to her elbows.

"You're going to continue your job here?" He wondered why, since her cover was blown. "I mean, now that your identity is out in the open?"

"I'm enjoying the horses." She swirled her fork through the whipped cream dusted with tinted sugar. "I didn't realize how much I missed the Arabian of my youth until I got into the barns here. And, as it turns out, I really believe in the ranch mission."

"The sustainable ranching?" Devon had spoken to a few of the Mesa Falls owners about that when he'd first arrived. Creating public awareness of the green initiatives on the land was the number one goal of the launch event that Salazar Media had been charged with executing.

He was drawn to the authenticity in her voice as she spoke, the passion for a cause he felt strongly about, as well.

"Yes." Regina moved one of the red taper candles out of the way so they could see each other better across the small table. "I know the practices aren't feasible for all ranches yet, but the more we learn about what works, the more we can incorporate holistic ranching ideas into livestock management everywhere. Someone has to go first."

"Agreed." He sipped the rich red port from a dessert wine glass. "You sound as prepared as anyone on my staff to write the talking points for the launch party speeches."

She laughed lightly, the candlelight catching deep shades of cherry in her dark hair. "I studied hard to convince the ranch manager that I was the one for the job. And as for my identity being in the open, are you sure you want it to be?"

"What do you mean?" Defensiveness had him sitting straighter in his seat.

"Georgiana Fuentes being out of the public eye has allowed interest in A. J. Sorensen's book to fade away." She set her fork crossways on her plate and leaned back from the table. "Are you prepared for the renewed media focus?"

Was she threatening to expose him?

"No one knows my father wrote it," he reminded

her, treading carefully. "So public attention would likely be more problematic for you than for me, unless you plan to reveal Alonzo's identity as the author."

"Right now, I'm more concerned with finding my own answers before media interest clouds the path," she explained. "So I won't be sharing that information—for now. But if you feel the need to out me, I wish you would give me fair warning. Tabloid media can descend with shocking speed."

He could see her point. But she'd also skillfully reminded him that she could send *his* life into a tailspin at any given moment if she blew the whistle on the author. All the more reason he planned to stick close to her throughout his stay at Mesa Falls Ranch.

"I understand why you'd prefer to remain anonymous. I won't share your real name with anyone." He wanted to touch her, to draw her against him, but the conversation called to mind all the thorny issues between them.

The mistrust.

"Thank you." She wrapped her arms around her midsection, the watchfulness in her gray eyes mirroring how he felt.

Dammit.

He reached for her in spite of the wariness, drawn by the connection that remained even now. He dragged his chair closer, his knee bumping hers under the table.

"It wasn't my intention to remind you of something painful." Covering her hand with his, he squeezed her fingers. "I plan to share with you what I learn from my private investigator about my father's reasons for writing the book."

He hadn't pressed her about her endgame in coming to Montana, about deceiving him to get close to him. Was her goal simply to gain information, like she'd implied? Or was it revenge?

With her body close to his, her dark hair spilling loose over one shoulder, and her cheeks lightly pink from the warmth or the wine, Devon found it tough to imagine her setting him up for some kind of payback plot. Especially after the feverish way they'd come together earlier, like they were in the grip of something bigger than both of them.

"We could share our resources in that regard," she offered, taking a sip from her water glass while, just outside the windows beside them, the moon made an appearance above the trees. "The man I hired to find the author behind the pseudonym might have information that would help your investigator's efforts."

"I'm meeting her tomorrow. Should I ask her to contact you?" He hesitated. "For that matter, would you consider sharing your identity with her, if you trust her discretion?"

He could hardly renege on the agreement he'd just made, but no doubt Regina could help with April Stephens's efforts to follow the money trail from the book's profits.

She stared down at their joined hands for a moment before meeting his gaze. "As long as I can speak to her directly. Yes, that's fine."

He heard what she didn't say—that trust was going to come in degrees for both of them. It was the best he could expect, considering their tenuous relationship. He'd have to hope she didn't reveal his father as the author of the book—at least not in the weeks leading up to his mother's wedding. And she would have to trust him to keep her secrets and maintain her privacy under the new identity she'd worked hard to build.

"Of course." He let go of her hand and slid his arm around her shoulders, feeling the silky warmth of her hair as it brushed his sleeve. "I'll let you make the call on how much you feel comfortable sharing with her. Just know that whatever you can tell her will probably help speed things along."

"Believe me, no one wants answers as much as I do." The fierceness of the words matched the spark in her eyes. Perhaps she heard it, too, because she smiled belatedly, as if to soften the tone. "And now, as much as I hate to end our date, I really should get back to the bunkhouse for the night."

"You're more than welcome to stay here, if you prefer." He stroked her hair behind her ear so he could see her face better. "For that matter, there's a spare bedroom if you'd rather have your privacy."

There was a pale red mark on her neck, an abrasion from his cheek, he guessed. He smoothed a finger over it, regretting that he'd marred her skin while he'd been kissing her.

"Thank you, but my gear is at the bunkhouse. And it's surprisingly fun rooming with a bunch of

women. Sort of like the summer camp I never had."
She shrugged, a small grin playing at the corners of
her mouth. "Besides, I've got an ear to the ground
on what's happening around the ranch that way. And
from what you said about your father's relationship
with the owners of Mesa Falls, it sounds like there
might be more to learn about him right here in Montana."

Devon stilled, realizing that he'd allowed sex
to scramble his thoughts. He mentally rewound to
their conversation on their horseback ride the day
before when he'd told her as much. What else had
he revealed about his dad before he discovered her
true identity? Of course, he'd known to be cautious
around her, so he hadn't said anything sensitive. Still,
it caught him off guard how quick she was to zero
in on a detail like that.

He kissed her cheek to try to hide his momentary
surprise, still struggling to negotiate the balance between wanting her and maintaining his focus.

"Good thinking." He felt the small shiver go
through her and wanted to explore it. To undress
her all over again. But he would wait until they had
more time. "The sleigh driver has returned to the
ranch for the night, but I can bring you back in the
all-terrain vehicle."

All of the cabins on the property came with the
added convenience. But Devon's thoughts were far
from the corporate retreat's luxuries as he retrieved
Regina's coat and hat, and they dressed to back out
into the cold.

He couldn't help remembering her last observation of the night—that she planned to key in on his father's relationships with the ranch owners. There was no doubt that Regina was sharp and quick-witted. And very committed to unearthing the truth behind his father's book.

As was he.

Selfishly, he hoped that whatever they found wouldn't destroy the tentative truce they'd made tonight. But more important, he needed to make sure the truth didn't implode on him before his mother's Christmas wedding.

Seven

Seated in a private meeting room at the Mesa Falls Ranch guest lodge, April Stephens reviewed her notes as Devon Salazar continued talking.

She'd purposely taken a high-back leather chair facing away from the spectacular view of the Bitterroot Mountains. She might not have time to indulge in the outdoors again during this trip, and she didn't want to tempt herself with the sight of those peaks. Instead, she grounded herself in the space around her, the warmth of the crackling fire in the hearth and the calming decor. The meeting room was sleekly understated in pale grays and cream, the furnishings not detracting from the real visual interest of the snowcapped mountains outside the wall of windows.

Her client was paying her firm well, and she wouldn't disappoint him. She'd been fortunate to have this opportunity to work with a powerful and high-profile figure like Devon Salazar in the first place. Her agency's senior financial investigator had a death in the family and her boss hadn't wanted to turn down the business. He'd offered April a serious incentive on this case.

Crack the secrets of Alonzo Salazar and she'd get a promotion. That meant more money, more travel and more opportunities to escape the responsibilities of the smothering home life weighing her down more every day.

April would not fail. She'd maxed out her credit cards buying a few high-end outfits to get through this week, needing to look the part of a senior staffer.

Had that been pathetically self-indulgent? Or a wise act of self-care that would put her more at ease with the well-heeled crowd that could afford to stay in places like Mesa Falls Ranch? She didn't know. But the buttery soft wool of the jacket she was wearing made her feel like a million bucks. And it was a good thing, because she dreaded sharing some of her findings with Devon. What if he didn't like what he heard? Would he put a halt to the investigation?

Now, as he brought her up to date about "Regina Flores"—the woman April had warned him about—she took notes by hand on a legal pad. Apparently he'd uncovered the woman's real identity: she was none other than the elusive Georgiana Fuentes, living and working right here in Montana. Which was most certainly not a coincidence, given that Devon was researching his father's book.

The book that had ruined Georgiana's life.

April remembered the sudsy read well. *Hollywood Newlyweds* by A. J. Sorensen had been a huge bestseller at a time when April read anything and everything she could get her hands on. She'd gobbled that book up, and had followed the tabloid headlines afterward when the supposedly fictional story turned out to have a basis in real life.

But no one in the media had seen Georgiana in years. So for her to pop up here, using a fake identity and trying to get close to Devon, was about as ominous as April could imagine. Unfortunately, her client didn't seem to share her concern.

"Georgiana invited me to contact her directly?" April asked him now, glancing up at him from across the small conference table.

He was uncommonly handsome, tall and well built, with light brown hair and attractive green eyes. He had an easy manner that made him a natural leader—the kind of man people would want to follow. Not that she was in the market for romance—far from it. But if she had been?

Yum.

The fact that he'd taken a marketing start-up founded by two brothers and grown it to a globally recognized leader in the social media environment appealed to her on an intellectual level, as well. Studying business accounting and working in financial investigations had given her an appreciation for the savvy it took to do something like that.

"She prefers to be called 'Regina.' And, yes." He slid a paper across the table toward April, and she noticed how the sleeves of his black button-down were rolled up. "We would like to keep her real identity private. The longer Georgiana stays out of the spotlight, the more likely my father's connection to the book will, too."

The "we" was not lost on April. Something in his tone gave her the idea that he felt protective of the woman. Guilt, perhaps, since his father's book had sent Georgiana's life into a tailspin? Or was there something else at work?

She planned to proceed carefully with the woman.

"Certainly." She tucked the contact information into a file folder. "I'll reach out to her as soon as we're done here."

"So my father was paying for a nominee service to collect his royalties on *Hollywood Newlyweds*?" Devon asked, returning to the information she'd given him earlier in the meeting. He flipped through web search results on a tablet before spinning his screen to show her a few prominent agencies.

"Yes." She'd invested far more hours than she would bill him to confirm it. "He set up his pen name like a corporation and gave it a director. The company collected monies from the publisher, and the nominee service oversaw the transactions and made sure taxes were paid."

A nominee service was extremely expensive, but it provided an unparalleled level of privacy.

"But the service must have expired with my father's death?" Frowning, Devon set the tablet on the sleek birchwood table. "There was nothing about that in the will."

"The service was paid for in advance. Given the precautions Alonzo took in order to keep his name away from the novel, I suspect he left explicit instructions for the royalty income after his death." April had chased the lead as far as she could for now, but she wouldn't give up. "Arrangements for future disbursements may already be in place and you weren't aware because you aren't a beneficiary. The other possibility is that the nominee hasn't learned of your father's death yet."

"Months after the fact?" Devon sounded skeptical. He glanced up from his tablet, one dark eyebrow raised.

"It's conceivable your dad only needed to touch base with the service once a year at tax time." She hesitated before sharing her biggest concern, not wanting to give him any reason to shut down this job. "And while I'm prepared to keep searching for information, you should know that in my experience, searches like this uncover illegal activity about fifty percent of the time."

Even though she hadn't taken the lead on an investigation before this one, she'd been in the weeds on similar cases at her firm for two years. And although there were highly reputable nominee services, the industry attracted its share of the criminal element.

"I appreciate the warning." Devon shut off his tablet and leaned back in the chair across from her, the afternoon sun gilding his features. He templed his fingers together, propping his chin on them. "My father obviously had a secret life we knew nothing about, but I still hold out hope that he had more altruistic reasons for hiding that income."

"So you're certain you want me to keep searching?" she clarified, needing his blessing before she unearthed news that could be upsetting on a personal level, or that had the potential to stir legal interest in the case.

"Absolutely. Whatever my father was up to, I need to know about it. And the sooner the better, April, so if you are in need of additional resources, don't hesitate to come to me."

She felt the thrill of victory at his words. She still had the job. The doorway for that promotion remained open.

"Understood." Hope filling her, she closed the leather cover over her legal pad and laid her pen on top of it. "I'll contact Regina Flores first, then begin contacting the owners of Mesa Falls Ranch to explore their connection to your father."

"And you'll continue looking into the nominee service?" he prompted, his words reminding her that she was getting into dicey terrain.

That information was well protected.

"I'll do everything in my power to find answers for you," she vowed, knowing she had to make it work.

"Very good." Standing, he ended the meeting with a handshake. "I look forward to hearing from you."

As he left the room, April's gut knotted tighter. How would she shake information out of a nominee service that sold complete anonymity to its clients? Her better hope was prying answers from Regina/ Georgiana. Or the owners of Mesa Falls Ranch.

As she packed the file and her pen in her bag, April's gaze veered out the meeting room windows toward the mountains. One day, she'd have the kind of life that allowed her the freedom of wide open spaces and fewer responsibilities. A life where she didn't need to constantly walk the tightrope between taking care of her mom and hiding her mother's increasing trouble from the world.

Until then, she would just keep her focus on the task at hand. Starting with Regina Flores.

Three days after her night with Devon, Regina was keeping her eye out for him in the great room at the main lodge, knowing he'd arrive soon.

She'd just finished a snowshoe trek with a group of new ranch guests. Her duties as a trail guide had quickly expanded from leading horseback rides to hosting other winter activities on the trails. With the huge influx of guests arriving for the launch event this week, all of the staff had been tapped to work extra hours. Now, as she transitioned her group of guests from the snowshoe activity to a whiskey tasting party in the great room, she would finally have her first evening free since the sleigh ride with Devon.

"The bourbons are on the bar and the scotches are on the buffet," she explained to an older couple puzzling over where to go next in the growing crowd.

Fires burned brightly in fireplaces at either end of the post-and-beam-style room. A huge antler chandelier hung low over a game table already filling with guests comparing tasting notes on preprinted cards. A solo guitar player sat in a high-backed stool near a stuffed grizzly bear. The scent of barbecue from the hors d'oeuvres being offered by passing waiters mingled with fragrant woodsmoke.

Regina took a bottled water from a silver tub full of ice near the whiskey display. Her cheeks were warm from the change in temperature after being outdoors for hours. She looked around the room, and somehow felt Devon behind her even before she turned to see him standing by the bar.

Her pulse quickened at the sight of him.

He wore dark jeans and leather loafers, but unlike most of the other men wearing flannel shirts or sweaters, he'd paired his denim with a white button-down and a gray tailored jacket. He didn't need a tie to appear like a man in charge.

Three days hadn't done anything to dampen Regina's hunger for him. But she'd spent every one of those days reminding herself that she needed to be wary with a Salazar. That she couldn't simply follow a compelling attraction to him; they had a far more complicated relationship.

But right now, seeing him again, she could only think about what it had been like to be bracketed in his strong arms. To feel the intense passion. To melt under his kiss.

By the time he arrived at her side, her breathing was fast and shallow.

He leaned closer to speak words for her alone. "If I'd known it would be three days before I saw you again, I wouldn't have been so quick to let you leave my cabin."

A thrill shot through her—both at his nearness and at the idea that he'd missed her. Wanted her.

Her skin tingled with awareness and he hadn't even touched her.

"Buildup to your launch event is keeping all the staff busy." She opened her water and took a cooling sip. "I had no idea the ride two days ago would turn into an overnight event."

His gaze lingered on her lips. "I didn't know, either, or I would have signed up for it myself." The heat in his green eyes distracted her. It made her forget what they'd been discussing, even quieted her years-old need for revenge. The strong reaction he incited both tantalized and worried her. She couldn't afford to let her feelings distract her from her goal.

Around them, the strains of a cowboy folk melody, the clinking of glasses and rumbled laughter faded until she could only hear her own breath.

"Are you free now?" he asked, his hand landing lightly on the small of her back.

"I planned to meet with—" She lowered her voice. "That is, I have a call scheduled from our mutual contact twenty minutes from now."

She'd been trying to find a time to speak to the private investigator, eager to get back on track with what she'd come to Montana to accomplish.

"Of course." He nodded, his hand still on her back. "She told me she'd been trying to reach you. Until then, maybe we could step out into a quieter spot."

Capping her water, she let him guide her through the crowded room. A pair of younger women stopped her to thank her for helping them with the snowshoe trek—or possibly to ogle Devon—but eventually she and Devon emerged from the great room to head toward the saloon.

He bypassed the bar and continued down a hall that led to the bowling alley and screening room. The sound of an old Western film filled the corridor for a moment before he steered her into a den that functioned as a small library. The three natural log walls were covered with floor-to-ceiling bookshelves, while the fourth wall featured a stone fireplace flanked by tall, narrow windows. A painting of one of the original homes on the ranch dominated the space above the fireplace.

Regina set her water bottle on a side table and wandered toward the hearth, her eye grazing the collection of photographs on the mantel showcasing the development of the property from small working ranch to corporate guest facility. She noticed Devon had closed the door behind them. Not that it would necessarily deter guests who wanted to drop in, but most of the activity in the lodge was in the dining rooms and bars by this time of evening.

He joined her by the fireplace, his gaze following the direction of hers briefly before returning to her. The scent of old books and pine hung in the air, familiar and welcoming.

"Are you all right?" He tipped her chin up so she was looking into his concerned green eyes. "I didn't know how to read your retreat."

Her belly flipped at his careful scrutiny. At the feeling she thought she heard in his voice.

No doubt she was misreading him, seeing a level of emotion that wasn't there. She was only valuable to him because he wanted to keep his father's deeds on lockdown.

"I'm fine." Steeling herself, she ignored the fluttery sensations his touch inspired. "I told you, I got roped into leading a longer tour than I'd signed on for. I hadn't realized that accompanying the group to a local ski resort meant I'd be stuck there until the ranch bus picked everyone up the next day."

He regarded her thoughtfully.

"You're putting in a lot of hours," he said finally, his hand falling away. "Are you sure this pursuit of my father's motives is worth so much of your time?"

Even as she missed the feel of his fingers on her cheek, she felt indignation straighten her spine.

"I thought I made it clear to you the other night that finding out why Alonzo mined my family's secrets for his own gain is my number one priority?" The words came out with more bite than she'd intended, but it frustrated her to think Devon couldn't see how deeply the book had affected her.

How it had *hurt*.

"You have every right to know." His voice hummed along her nerve endings, seemingly calibrated to soothe her. "My point is that I can help you now. You don't need to do this alone anymore."

His calm, easy demeanor only reminded her that Devon had lived without any knowledge of his father's actions until recently, whereas she'd been keenly aware of them her whole life, even if she hadn't known whom to blame for them.

"Are you suggesting I give up my quest and go home?" With an effort, she held herself very still, ignoring the physical need to be close to him and restraining the impulse to run. "Trust that the son of someone who tore apart my family will turn out to be an ally?"

Frustration vibrated through her, making her limbs shaky while the sounds of the Western movie in the room next door briefly blared louder. A gunfight, maybe, with swelling, suspenseful music that hummed through the hardwood floor.

"Is that the real reason you've been avoiding me these last three days?" The muscle in Devon's jaw tensed. Flexed. "Because you're back to thinking of me as your enemy?"

"I never said that." Wrapping her arms around herself, she turned from the hearth to stare out the dark window at the stars dotting the horizon.

She recognized there could be a grain of truth in his accusation. She had gladly accepted the extra workload, telling herself she might have a chance to learn more about the elusive ranch owners who had a close relationship to Alonzo Salazar.

But was that the real reason she'd filled her calendar?

"You didn't need to." He remained by the crackling fire, his broad shoulders outlined by the orange glow. "And I understand if you want to pursue answers in your own way. But my offer still stands to share information and resources. April Stephens is going to get to the bottom of this faster than you or I could alone."

Regina bit her lip to keep herself from responding impulsively. Angrily. Yet the injustice of the situation wouldn't let her stay quiet.

"Her allegiance is to you, because you're paying her." She'd had a lot of time to think about it these past few days when she'd buried herself in the work of entertaining guests. "And you have to recognize the extreme financial disconnect between our stations in life right now. You're running a successful business, possibly funded by your father's ill-gotten gains. I'm seasonal ranch help after being disowned by my father thanks to your dad."

"That's not fair." Devon stalked closer, taking a

breath as if he was about to expound on the point, but she held up a hand to forestall him.

"I realize that," she conceded, her pulse speeding up again when he closed the distance between them. "Your business has grown because of your talent and commitment. I've meandered around without a solid career direction. That's on me."

A log in the fire slipped, spewing embers and hissing softly.

"But you feel robbed of opportunities, while they've been handed to me?" He shook his head. "If my father had access to hidden wealth, he never spent it on his sons."

"Yet he was an investor in Salazar Media." She'd looked it up and the amount was staggering. "It's a matter of public record."

Devon's lips flattened into a line for a moment as he studied her. She wanted to reach out and touch his shadowed jaw, even when she felt an unreasonable resentment.

"True." He nodded in a distracted way, his gaze sliding from hers to peer into the distance. "Though the amount was funded from his retirement account. I worried about him giving us that money because it meant he'd have nothing to live on while waiting for the company to start turning a profit."

Turning on his heel, Devon paced away from her, clearly caught up in his own thoughts. It seemed that he was speaking to himself more than her.

"What is it? Did you remember something?"

She knew he didn't have to tell her. But maybe

she'd catch him in an unguarded moment. Hadn't he just been asking her to trust him to share with her?

She followed him toward the sofa table that held a stone statue of a bucking bronc.

"Dad traveled a lot." Devon slid a sideways glance toward her. "Friends who knew about those trips used to joke that he must be a secret agent on the side."

"Trips where?" Anticipation curled through her that she might learn something.

And yet, would discovering the truth about the father alienate her from the son forever? It shouldn't matter to her. Except after what she'd shared with Devon at his cabin, she couldn't deny that it would.

"We didn't know." Devon faced her, the warmth of his body suddenly close to hers. "Since finding out about the novel, I thought maybe he was just seeking out quiet places to write."

"But now you're wondering if he was financing a more extravagant lifestyle you didn't know about?" A piece of her hoped that Devon truly wasn't aware of that hidden income.

"Not necessarily." He withdrew his phone from his jacket pocket and tapped in a note. "It's occurred to me that the investigator would surely be able to track some of those travel dates. Perhaps his destinations on those trips would provide more insights."

Regina chewed on that idea while he finished typing. No doubt he had a good point. She felt uneasy that she hadn't spoken to the investigator herself yet. What if she held the missing pieces of the Alonzo Salazar puzzle?

Nearby a wall clock chimed the hour.

"Speaking of which, I'm scheduled to talk to her now." She needed to get her own read on April Stephens and decide how much she could trust the investigator. "I don't want to miss her again."

Devon deposited his cell into his jacket pocket. "If you'd like this room, I can give you privacy. I need to go over some particulars on the launch event with the ranch manager."

"Thank you." She retrieved her water bottle from where she'd set it on a side table earlier. "That would work well. If anyone comes in, I can always take the call outside."

"Can I take you out tomorrow night?" he asked quietly, his green eyes darkening.

An answering shiver ran up her spine as her body reminded her how much she'd like that.

"Because you want to see me?" she asked, tempted, but needing to keep a level head around this man. "Or because you want to keep an eye on me?"

"I could ask you the same question about why you spend time with me," he reminded her, angling closer in a way that made her heart skip a beat.

Or two.

When his lips closed over hers, she didn't hesitate to kiss him back. The kiss was slow, thorough and sensual. A deliberate reminder of what it was like between them. Her arms wrapped around his waist, fingers curling into his shirt as hunger returned with an aching insistence.

As her breasts tightened, her nipples peaked

against the fabric of her bra. She almost forgot everything else until he pulled away, his breathing ragged.

"You decide what you want next, Regina." His hands slid away from her, and it was all she could do to remain upright. "I want you, but only when you're sure about this. About me."

She blinked fast, trying to think of a response, but he was already walking away. He closed the door to the den behind him, leaving her beside the hearth while the fire blazed.

Regina bit her lip until it hurt and waited for her thoughts to reassemble themselves. For reason to return. She was turned on. Confused.

And very, very alone.

Eight

An hour later, Regina sat in a deep leather barrel chair kitty-corner to April Stephens in the Mesa Falls Ranch den.

The investigator had asked to meet in person once she'd discovered that Regina was at the main lodge, and within five minutes of the call, the two of them had taken seats next to one of the tall windows flanking the fireplace.

April defied every expectation Regina had of a female PI. The willowy blonde's long hair hung in full curls around the shoulders of a suit that looked right out of the pages of a fashion magazine. From her stilettos to her French manicure, April appeared more apt to step out of a limo on Park Avenue than sit in a stakeout. But maybe that was because her investigative specialty was financial forensics.

Now, taking notes in longhand on a legal pad, April paused to peer up at Regina.

"Did your mother ever speculate about who in her life might have betrayed her trust?" The woman had listened without interruption while Regina recounted growing up as Georgiana Cameron, daughter of the prominent film star, before getting iced out of her "father's" life once the scandal broke involving *Hollywood Newlyweds*. She should have been numbed to telling by now, but sharing about the betrayal still left her raw and vulnerable, perhaps because she was still unsettled by her last conversation with Devon.

A burst of applause erupted in a room nearby, then died down again. The entertainment areas of the lodge had remained busy throughout the evening, but no one else had entered the den except for a passing waiter who'd asked if they needed anything. Regina sipped her water and set it back on the small round table with a wagon wheel painted on it, which sat between their chairs. Her hand trembled enough to give away her fractured emotions, and she yanked it back fast.

"She said the only people who knew about her affair with my birth father were her two best friends and their yoga instructor." Regina hadn't thought back to that in a long time, and she appreciated April coming at the story with fresh eyes. But would it help Regina in the long run, or only serve Devon? "Eventually, Mom decided it must have been my father who'd let it slip to someone, because she trusted all of those women implicitly."

"Have your mom's friends ever been questioned?" April shifted in her chair, the red soles of her shoes flashing for a moment as she recrossed her slim legs. "By a professional investigator, that is?"

"No." Regina felt a surge of hope that maybe something could still be unearthed from one of them. "I'm the only member of my family who has ever paid anyone to look into the matter, and I didn't have the budget for it that Devon Salazar does."

"Will it create discomfort for your family if I question your mother's friends now?" April asked, pen hovering in midair over her paper while she waited for an answer.

"Not at all." She withdrew her phone and started typing in names. "I'll send you their contact information, but I should warn you that I've spoken to all of them before." Although, looking back on those conversations, she remembered how emotional she'd been at the time. It had been shortly after her high school graduation, when the realization had settled in that her life would never, ever, be the same again. "Come to think of it, they were probably all hesitant to share anything with me based on how personally involved I was. Am."

April remained quiet for a moment while Regina looked up phone numbers and emails, drawing comfort in the task, feeling proactive for once, rather than just reactive. Once Regina sent April the text with all the info, the investigator spoke again.

"I'm going to get to the bottom of it," she said, blue eyes unwavering, voice certain. "We'll have answers soon."

In that moment, Regina saw beyond the pretty, carefully cultivated exterior to the fierceness beneath.

And she believed her.

"I look forward to that."

They spoke for another quarter of an hour, going over details of Regina's past before wrapping up the interview. She assured April she'd never met Alonzo Salazar or even heard of him before her own PI finally turned up the name earlier in the year. When the woman seemed satisfied she had enough answers, the two of them parted ways. April strode out of the den on her elegant high heels while Regina stood on shaky legs to return to the bunkhouse for the night. She wanted to believe it was just weariness from snowshoeing, but it more likely had to do with dredging up the past. She didn't know if she could trust her feelings for Devon. Or his for her.

Strangely, April Stephens had seemed like an ally even though she worked for Devon. That was only an illusion, though, and Regina would be foolish to think otherwise. The investigator would have allegiance to the man who'd hired her—end of story. Which meant Regina needed to stay close to that man if she wanted to know what April turned up.

That had been her plan all along and, pride be damned, she was going to stick to it because she was finally getting close to having answers about Alonzo Salazar and his book.

Regina told herself that was why she was seeing Devon again tomorrow night. It didn't have anything to do with being wildly attracted to him.

If Devon had been an oddsmaker, he would have put the likelihood of seeing Regina tonight at 50 percent.

After the way she'd avoided him for days, then danced around the idea of meeting, he feared her conflicted feelings about their relationship had over-shadowed the attraction.

Then, in the middle of a meeting with his planning committee for the Mesa Falls launch event, he'd spotted her text asking if they could get together.

"This was a fun surprise." Regina's face glowed in the firelight as she passed him an old-fashioned tin star for the top of the Christmas tree in his cabin. "I never guessed you would choose tree-decorating for a date night. Where did you get the ornaments?"

They were seated on the couch in the living area. Instrumental Christmas tunes played over the room's built-in speaker system, and the white tree lights glowed on the fresh balsam, which was tucked in the corner between the bookshelves and a wingback.

Regina's red sweater had a V-neck that framed a necklace of tiny silver jingle bells, and a slim black skirt hugged her curves in a way that drew his eye every time she moved. Her dark hair was pinned back in a green-and-red plaid bow. She seemed more relaxed tonight than when they'd spoken in the lodge the night before. The jasmine scent of her fragrance wafted under the stronger smell of pine in the room.

"I ordered the box last week from a charity I work with in New York. They provide everything you need for themed trees, and half the cost goes to holiday gifts for people in need." He set aside the star to save for the end. "To be honest, I was going to have my staff decorate for a photo op to post on social media. But when you messaged me, I thought it might be fun for us to tackle."

She grinned as she pulled a straw cowboy hat ornament from the box. "You must have chosen the Western theme."

"The official name is 'Cowboy Christmas.'" He peered into the box on the coffee table, full of rodeo-themed decorations along with a garland made of twine and tiny reproduction horseshoes. "I thought it would work well with the cabin's design."

"Are they a client of yours?" She sipped the champagne cocktail he'd made for her. Her silver bangle clinked against the base of the flute as she set it back on the table.

His gaze lingered on the long spill of her dark hair on her shoulder as she moved. He wanted to touch the strands, to breathe in the fragrance of the silky mass. To taste the delicate column of her neck.

But he was trying his damnedest to give her some space. To let her set the pace tonight after the way she'd seemed skittish about continuing their relationship.

"You could say that." He stood up to keep himself from following the impulse to touch her. Digging the garland out of the box, he started wrapping it around the tree limbs. "From the inception of the business, my brother and I wanted to allocate a percentage of company resources to community giving. The organization that sells the ornament boxes was just getting started in New York at the same time we were, so we approached them to see if they wanted some help."

The holiday music switched to a country tune, with steel guitars and more folksy vocals. Devon stood back to see how the garland looked while Regina joined him near the tree. Growing up, he had never decorated a tree with his family. In his grandfather's palatial mansion, trees simply appeared one day, professionally trimmed. Even as an adult, he'd found his decorating opportunities were limited to office parties, as a way to connect with his staff. But something had made him want to share this with Regina tonight. Maybe a sense that her family holidays had to have been painful after her parents' well-publicized split.

"That was good of you." There was a wistful note in her voice as she slid a velvety quarter horse decoration onto a branch. "You've accomplished so much between growing your business and giving back." She straightened the ornament, so the horse dangled the way she wanted it to. "And during that same amount of time, I feel like all I've accomplished is chasing my tail."

Regret for what she'd gone through rained over him. How could his father have published that damned book and destroyed her family?

"This week is going to mark a turning point for you, though." He couldn't help but touch her then, needing to reassure her. His hand went to the space between her narrow shoulder blades. "Once you have the answers you deserve, you'll be ready to move forward."

Her angora sweater was impossibly soft. Even so, he remembered that it didn't compare to the texture of the creamy skin beneath it. Thoughts of stripping her naked forced him to move his hand away again.

"I hope so." She found more ornaments to hang and they worked in tandem for a few minutes. "Have you heard from April?" Her gaze flicked over to his.

Wariness crept through him.

Was this why she'd wanted to see him tonight?

But then, he told himself it was only natural she'd want to know. He'd just told her she'd have answers soon, after all.

"She took a red-eye to the West Coast last night." He met Regina's surprised gaze. "To follow up on leads you gave her, apparently."

Devon hadn't asked the PI for details. His work-days had been crammed with the logistics of the ranch's launch event. He had a sizable staff on hand in Montana now, but the event included satellite parties taking place simultaneously on both coasts in real time. This would allow Mesa Falls Ranch to reach more potential clients, even if the expenses were high up front. Bottom line, he needed staffing in both cities, coordinating everything.

"Wow. That was fast." Regina held a pewter ornament shaped like a pair of cowboy boots in mid-air, as if she'd forgotten what she was doing. "I'm grateful for your support in helping her get to the bottom of this."

Something about the way she said it rankled. He took the boots from her and found a spot for them on the tree, then cupped her shoulders in his hands.

"I need answers as much as you do. It's not just kindness. It's good business to work together." He didn't want her gratitude. And damn it, he sure didn't want to think that she was only spending time with him for the sake of the investigation.

Her brows knitted together as she frowned. "In that case, thanks for doing business with me."

He shook his head, letting go of her. "Are you always so prickly, or is it just me who brings out the defensive side?"

Her sudden burst of laughter smoothed over his irritation, the sound far more melodious than anything playing on the Christmas music station.

"Maybe a little of both. I definitely have prickly down to an art." She bent closer to the coffee table and retrieved her champagne flute for another sip of her drink, the bubbles glowing golden in the firelight.

"And why is that?" he asked, genuinely curious about her.

"After the whole debacle of the book—and losing my old friends—it became a protective measure, maybe. It was just easier to keep people at arm's length rather than let anyone close enough to hurt me again." She set aside the flute and studied the tree. "And I've only started to recognize that tendency this week, as I grow closer to some of the women in my bunkhouse. It makes me realize I've gone a lot of years without friends."

The acknowledgement of her solitary existence saddened him as she took time rearranging a few of the tree lights so they illuminated some of the ornaments from behind.

"Will you go home for Christmas?" He hated to think about her remaining at the ranch during a time most people spent with their families.

She shrugged in a way that shifted the neckline of her sweater closer to the edge of one shoulder.

"It depends how much progress I make in finding answers about your dad and the book." Spinning to face him, she seemed to notice his careful regard, and her cheeks flushed a deeper pink. "If I think that staying here over the holidays will give me opportunities to speak to any of the owners privately, then I will stick around."

He wanted to reassure her. To give her some concrete findings from April's investigation that would ease Regina's fierce desire for the truth.

But what if giving her those answers meant she would turn on him? Would she sue his father's estate for defamation or drag the Salazar name through the tabloids?

When he didn't reply right away, she leaned past him to retrieve a package of ornament hooks. "What about you?" she asked. "What are you doing for the holidays?"

"My mother is getting married on Christmas Eve." Tension pulled his shoulders tight, the way it had all week when he thought about the wedding. Because his meeting with the PI—her warning that Alonzo hiding his money could indicate illegal activity—made Devon worry how soon something would leak about his father's hidden life. "I'm flying to Connecticut to be with her right after the launch party."

"That should be fun, right?" Regina's jingle bell necklace chimed softly as she moved to decorate the left side of the tree.

His gaze followed her movements as the tree's golden glow lit up her features. Thinking about the wedding forced him to consider what his life would be like once he left Mesa Falls and Regina behind. And the vision made him feel suddenly empty.

"It would be more fun with a date." He articulated the idea the moment it came into his head. Because why not? He'd started this relationship to keep an eye on her.

Just because it had grown into more than that didn't mean that the need to keep her closer had dissipated. Far from it. If she had any inclination to drag his father's book back into the public spotlight for some sort of payback scheme, he'd prefer to know about it sooner rather than later.

"Are you asking me to attend the wedding with you?" She frowned, clearly surprised.

Because she was ready for their time together to end? Or because she hadn't expected this relationship to continue after he left Montana?

"I am." He stepped closer, breathing her in. "I can already tell I'm not going to be able to walk away after the launch event."

She licked her lips. "Can I think it over?"

"Of course." He wasn't going to press her, especially since the wedding would mean spending Christmas together. "I need to fly out right after the launch party for some pre-wedding festivities. But my mother gets married on Christmas Eve, so you could wait and join me the next day."

She gave a thoughtful nod, lips pressed in a flat line. "Do you like the guy she's marrying?"

"I don't know him that well," he admitted. That was partly his fault for not making more of an effort, but also because his grandfather had claimed all the family's face time with the groom-to-be in order to strengthen Radcliffe ties with the international banker. "But I think having someone marry your mother is like someone marrying a daughter— no one will ever be good enough for her in my eyes."

Regina bent to decorate a lower branch. "That's a touching sentiment from a son." Her expression turned strained as she straightened. "Or a father, for that matter." She busied herself, adjusting things she'd already tidied. "Did you spend much time with your father as a kid?"

"No." His role model had been his cold and distant grandfather, who'd made sure Devon knew he would never be good enough because he wasn't a Radcliffe. "I visited the West Coast a couple times to see him, but mostly my mother insisted he come back East if he wanted a relationship with me."

As a teacher—even in an elite private boarding school—Alonzo had never had much money when Devon was younger. Later in life, when Devon was in his late teens, his father had had noticeably more disposable income. Now Devon knew that was thanks to *Hollywood Newlyweds*.

"What was he like?" She wandered over to the side table, where Devon had put out the offerings from the chef to accompany the champagne.

Plucking a dark salted caramel from a small silver tray, she nibbled on it as she watched him.

"An inspiring teacher." Devon had heard it over and over again throughout his life, and especially after the funeral, when former students began sending condolences. "He wasn't an involved father to my brother or me, and he didn't place any importance on marriage as an institution, which hurt more than one of the women he loved." He watched Regina's tongue sweep away a tiny spot of caramel on her upper lip, the movement igniting a fresh blaze of desire for her. "But he made a difference in the lives of his students and that meant something to him."

He forced himself to focus on decorating the tree to keep from touching her. Tasting her.

He'd been so damned determined to let this night

move more slowly. To allow her to dictate how things went. But he'd forgotten the potent power of Regina's appeal.

"I read about that boarding school online." She retrieved a Santa dressed in chaps and spurs from the box and went back to the tree, her curves drawing Devon's eye as she moved past. "Dowdon isn't all that far from Hollywood in miles, but it might as well be on the other side of the globe for how much the community differs from the social scene portrayed in his book."

Devon had thought the same thing. "One of the school's biggest selling points is the remote location in a national forest, close to a protected wilderness area."

As a kid, he'd thought it sounded idyllic. His father lived on the campus, and was part of the horse program, which offered a mount to every student for the duration of their time at Dowdon. Learning to ride, caring for an animal and competing in horsemanship activities were all central to the experience.

"I wonder if he could have met my mother somehow." Regina's silver-gray gaze locked with Devon's. "He obviously knew a great deal about her private life."

Devon heard the resentment leak into her voice, and hoped to reroute the conversation before it turned more divisive.

"What's your mom like?" he asked to distract her. "I remember some of her films."

For a few years, Tabitha Barnes had been the

queen of romantic comedies, but she'd stopped making movies after her affair began dominating headlines.

"Bubbly. Sweet." Regina seemed to take the question seriously, a slow smile spreading over her features. "Not all that different from the characters she played during her filmmaking heyday. Davis—the man I believed to be my dad for the first fifteen years—fell in love with her when he was making his directorial debut. He starred in the picture that was her breakout movie, and he directed it, too."

Devon thought he detected a begrudging pride in those words, and he recalled that talk about Davis Cameron hurt her most. No doubt because the man had cut ties so completely.

"It was unnecessarily cruel of him to push you out of his life." How could a grown man purposely distance himself from a daughter he'd raised as his own? From what Devon could gather, Regina had been close to Davis Cameron—perhaps even closer than she was to her mother. "In all the years since he ended things with your mom, has he ever contacted you?"

"Never." The answer sounded like it came from a ripped-raw place, but she cleared her throat and moved purposely back toward the box of ornaments. "At least he's been consistent about not talking to the media, either. There was a small amount of comfort in the fact that he never commented on the situation."

"I'm sorry I brought it up," Devon told her sincerely, intercepting her before she could pull more ornaments from the box. "I can't imagine how painful it was for you to have your world turned upside down by that damned book. But I'm confident we'll hear from April soon with some more definitive answers."

He took her hand in his, folding her fingers into his palm.

"The mystery behind *Hollywood Newlyweds* has dominated my life for years." She shook her head and huffed out a sigh, sounding upset. "And I'm not very good at putting the frustrations out of my mind once I start thinking about it. The resentment just festers."

He drew her closer, wishing he could absorb the hurt and take away that pain. His father had no business tearing apart her family or making them the center of public speculation for years. Devon wanted to make amends.

And right now, he had an idea how he could help, at least temporarily.

"Maybe you should let me distract you." He lowered his lips to her ear to speak softly against her skin. "Give you something else to think about."

Already, his heart hammered with wanting her. When she sucked in a sharp breath, the need for her multiplied exponentially.

"I thought you said I was too prickly and defensive," she reminded him, arching a dark eyebrow as she gazed up at him. "Are you sure you want to tangle with me?"

There was a light, teasing note in her voice, but Devon suspected she'd put it there to mask a moment of insecurity and doubt. Not that he'd let her see he recognized it for what it was.

A vulnerability.

So he skimmed his hands around her shoulders and sifted through the silky dark hair.

"It would be the greatest pleasure I can imagine."

Nine

Every day that Regina had been without Devon felt like years, making her question how she'd stayed away from him for this long.

Winding her arms around his neck, she sighed into him, letting go of all the excellent reasons she had for not trusting him. Tonight, he'd showed her a new level of caring, a kindness even more compelling than the red-hot attraction between them.

She lost herself in his kiss, his tongue sweeping over hers in a way that made her forget everything but him. How was that even possible?

But she didn't want to ruminate or overanalyze. Right now, when she had the chance to forget all the old wounds, to shut out everything else but this moment with Devon Salazar, she would embrace it.

His hands skimmed her curves, stirring pleasure. She arched closer, remembering how he could make her feel. How good they were together.

She broke the kiss, determined to make her desires clear. Breathing hard, she stared up into his green eyes that were so intent. So hungry.

"I'll take all the distraction you can give," she whispered, her voice a husky rasp of sound, before she turned and led him toward the bedroom she remembered well.

He caught up to her in a half step, plucking her off her feet and lifting her in his arms like a groom carrying a new bride over the threshold. Squealing in surprise, she shoved aside the romantic thought. His hold on her gave her the chance to appreciate his broad chest, though. She ran her hand over one muscular shoulder.

He entered the master suite, kicking the door shut with his foot, his focus on the bed in the center of the room. Her focus was all for him as she trailed kisses along the underside of his neck. She traced with her tongue, for only a moment, the place where his pulse leaped, before he set her on the bed with a bounce.

She toed off her shoes while he raked his shirt up and off, his movements visible in the light from sconces on either side of the mantel. He was built like a swimmer, tall with wide shoulders and a body that tapered to lean hips. Her gaze dipped lower as he flicked open the fastening on his jeans. She couldn't concentrate on her own undressing in her desire to watch him. The narrow line of dark hair disappearing under the cotton of his boxers tempted her to touch him there. But when she reached for him, he caught her wrist in a surprisingly strong hold.

"I really like what you're thinking." He loosened his grip as he pushed her back on the mattress, her head sinking into a down pillow. The jingle bells on her necklace slid along her neck to fall onto the bed behind her. "But it's supposed to be me who distracts you. Not the other way around."

"How do you know what I was thinking?" She tugged the bow from her hair, then smoothed her hands over his chest, savoring the warmth of his skin.

"I didn't. I only knew I liked it." He lowered himself enough to kiss the patch of flesh bared by her sweater, taking his time to taste the lowest point of the V-neck. "There was something a little bit wicked in the way you were looking at me."

He nuzzled her sweater off one shoulder, then clamped his teeth on one black silk bra strap, dragging it down. An ache started between her thighs as he let go of the silk and reared back on his knees to look at her.

Their eyes met. Held.

Was there more between them than heat and hunger?

A moment later, he peeled off her sweater and bra, letting them fall to one side of the bed. He cupped her breasts, tasting each one in turn, teasing the taut peaks. When he drew one into his mouth, suckling, the hunger for him grew unbearably. She arched her hips into him, needing more. Now.

He slid her skirt over her curves, and the rush of lust made her dizzy. His hands skimmed her inner thighs before dragging her panties down and off. She twisted the fabric of the duvet between her fingers, muttering wordless pleas for more.

By the time his lips covered her sex, she was so close to release she had all she could do to hold on another moment, allowing the intense, heady pleasure to build more as his tongue traced her.

She let go of the duvet as his shoulder dipped beneath her thigh, positioning her where he wanted her. The stubble on his jaw rubbing lightly against her thigh proved the tipping point, the feeling so exquisitely sensual she went hurtling into a lush, endless orgasm.

Ripples of pleasure pulsed through her, over and over. She let the sensations have their way with her as her whole body seized with bliss. While she gathered her breath, Devon moved over her, standing to shed the rest of his clothes. She soaked in the sight of him, her heart pounding madly while he found a condom and rolled it into place.

He stretched out over her just long enough for her to feel the thrill of anticipation all over again. When he entered her, she wrapped her legs around his waist. Holding him there. Moving with him in a rhythm all their own.

She streaked her fingers through his hair, kissing everywhere she could reach. Nibbling. Biting gently. Then he took over the kiss, his hips and tongue moving in a tantalizing sync.

They rolled over once. Trading the top position, letting each other lead the way. It was all delicious. Exciting. So much more than she'd ever experienced before in a relationship.

Devon's breath went ragged and she closed her eyes, feeling how close he was in the tension along his shoulders. His hips rocked hard into her, the pressure stroking a place inside her that unleased a fresh wave of release. Pleasure uncoiled, and her body quivered from it. She knew the movement pushed him over the edge, too, his spine arching, his breathing turning harsh.

After long moments, they collapsed side by side, limbs tangled. She tipped her forehead into his chest, feeling the comforting thunder of his heartbeat before it slowed by degrees. Eventually, her skin cooled. Her inhalations slowed along with her pulse. But through it all, Devon's arms remained wrapped around her, holding her close.

A long, shuddering sigh left her, and she knew she could gladly remain tucked against him the whole night through.

As long as she didn't let herself think about what had brought them to this moment. His promise to distract her. Her willingness—gratitude, even—for his ability to give her that.

Devon stroked her hair from her face, his touch soothing her before her anxieties could ratchet up again. She told herself she could remain here another minute to soak up the sensation that felt close to…tenderness.

It was wholly unexpected.

And simultaneously undeniable.

She sat up, knowing she didn't dare indulge something that could come back to bite her in the long run. Devon straightened beside her, his expression puzzled. But before he could ask her anything, his cell phone vibrated on the nightstand table.

Once. Twice.

She felt relieved when he turned to glance at it. But some of the relief faded as he punched a button on the screen.

"It's April," he informed Regina a moment before speaking into the device. "Salazar here. April, I'm going to put you on speaker so Regina can hear whatever news you have to share."

Devon didn't normally make impulsive decisions. But he needed Regina to start trusting him if he wanted to get to the bottom of his father's secrets. Sharing the PI's findings with her seemed like a way to show her he was serious about uncovering the truth. And that he was as much in the dark about his dad's motives as she was.

The surprise in her silver-gray eyes as she sat up in bed told him that she hadn't expected this kind of primary access to the private investigator. He hoped it was a step in the right direction to winning Regina over. Because as his gaze fell to her bare shoulders visible above the duvet she held to her chest, he felt a surge of protectiveness toward her. A need to make sure nothing else hurt her.

Now April's voice sounded through the speaker on his cell phone as he held it between them.

"I'm still searching for answers about how Alonzo got access to Tabitha Barnes's story in the first place," April told them. "But I have one more interview with her yoga instructor tomorrow before I fly back to Montana."

Devon studied Regina's profile as she listened. Her shoulders were tense. She chewed her lip, still pink from his kiss.

"Maybe that will yield something," he remarked, if only to reassure Regina. "Any other news?"

"Yes, actually." April's cool, professional tone gave nothing away. "I discovered Alonzo's destination for many of his secret trips."

Regina's gaze flew to Devon's. She reached to grab his wrist. Was she hopeful? Nervous? Maybe a little of both.

"And?" he prodded, even as his stomach rebelled at the idea of his father being implicated in any wrongdoing. It was bad enough he'd written the book that hurt Regina in the first place.

"He frequently visited a cabin in Kalispell, Montana, that belonged to a woman I believe was a romantic interest." April paused, and in that moment of quiet, his phone chimed with a new notification. "I just sent you her contact information."

More women in his father's life. No real surprise there, since Alonzo had once told Devon's mother that he thought marriage "killed the creative spirit." Alonzo had long considered himself a lover and admirer of women in general, but never one in particular.

And damn, but Devon needed to keep Alonzo Salazar's name out of the public eye until after his mother's wedding. His mom didn't need any of the old frustrations resurfacing now. His father's choices might have soured Devon on relationships, but that didn't mean he couldn't applaud his mother's ability to find faith in love.

Beside him, Regina let go of his wrist, and the loss of her touch frustrated him. It reminded him she was going to slip away, too, if he couldn't figure out how and why his father had written the tell-all book about her family.

He glanced down at the incoming text on his cell.

"Fallon Reed." Devon read the name aloud where it flashed on his screen. "I don't remember him ever mentioning her."

He looked to Regina, but she shook her head.

"The email I sent to her came back with a notification that the account no longer exists, but I'll drive to Kalispell to speak to her if I have to." The investigator shuffled some papers on her end of the call. "But Ms. Reed is significant because she's related to one of the owners of Mesa Falls Ranch."

"Which one?" Regina asked before Devon could. Her fingers clenched the duvet cover again, dragging it higher against her bare body.

Devon could feel her anxiety in the way her muscles coiled as she went still.

"My mistake. Make that a relation to *two* of the owners," April corrected herself. "Fallon Reed is an aunt to Weston and Miles Rivera."

"Is there any reason to think this woman profited from Alonzo's novel?" Regina asked, her voice tinged with worry.

Or was it defensiveness? Restrained anger?

Whatever the emotion behind the question was, Devon could tell it was intense. She bit her lip, breathing hard.

"Not as of yet." April's tone was cautious, as if she didn't completely rule the idea out. "Tracing the payments from the book is proving difficult, as I explained to Devon."

He felt Regina's gaze land on him. Was the look in her eyes accusatory?

Something about her expression struck him as frustrated, almost as if he'd betrayed her.

April went on to outline her next steps—interview the yoga instructor, return to Montana, then speak to Weston Rivera and possibly visit Fallon Reed. Devon only half listened as she bade them good-night, however. He was more concerned with Regina's reaction that he couldn't quite read.

By the time he disconnected the call, Regina was sliding out of bed, wrapping a chenille throw around her shoulders.

"Where are you going?" He grabbed his pants and stepped into them, wondering what he'd missed.

"I thought you were sharing the information from this investigation?" She lost no time retrieving her skirt and sweater.

"I am." He followed her until she disappeared into the en suite bath, where he stopped outside the partially closed door. "That's why I took the call with you, so you could hear what's going on."

What was she upset about? He could hear her rustling around in there while he searched for his shirt.

"Yet you never mentioned one word to me about tracing payments from the book, let alone why it was proving difficult." She flung the investigator's words back at him before she emerged from the bathroom with her clothes back in place.

Her hair fell loose around her shoulders now. He also thought her sweater might be inside out, but he said nothing about that, seeing the emotions blaze in her eyes.

She really thought he was hiding things from her.

"There was nothing to tell," he reminded her, trying to put himself in her position. Trying to understand how she could be so defensive so fast. "You heard that for yourself from April."

"I disagree." Pivoting on her heel, she stalked out of the bedroom and back into the cabin's living area. "You could have explained to me why there is a holdup," she said even as she barreled around the room, finding her bag to toss her hair bow into it. "We could have had a conversation about why it's difficult, or you could have shared the obstacles with me. But I am in the dark, Devon. As I always have been where your father's motives are concerned."

"Whoa." He saw her silhouetted in front of the Christmas tree where they'd been having fun decorating just an hour ago. "Let me tell you now—I understand how important it is to you."

It hadn't been his intention to hide significant parts of the investigation. And it saddened him to see how carefully she needed to weigh his words. To test them for truth.

No question about it, Regina had been hurt before.

He reached out to brush a touch along her shoulder. Gently. Carefully.

"Give me a chance," he said, not sure when it had become so important that she let him in. But somehow, it had. "If you don't like what I have to say, I'll make sure you get back to the bunkhouse safely. Okay?"

Another interminable moment passed. In the end, she nodded.

He reached for the remote on the side table to shut off the holiday tunes. With the room quiet and Regina listening, he shared what April had told him about his father hiring a nominee service to collect the payments from the publisher to A. J. Sorensen. Briefly, he explained how they worked, based on the research he'd done since then.

"Apparently, Dad contracted a nominee through a lawyer, which gave him attorney-client privilege, as well." He'd read over April's notes more carefully after their meeting to discover that, learning how it gave his father's pseudonym an added level of privacy.

Regina folded her arms around herself, her brows knitting in thought. She paced past him, setting her purse back on the couch now that she wasn't heading out the door.

He was relieved about that. Grateful to have her stay. And damn it, he wanted to get to the bottom of what his father had been doing—for her sake and, yes, for his own, as well. He just wished the timing had been better since he couldn't afford for the truth to come out now.

"So the nominee service is still active," she mused. "And still covered by the attorney-client privilege." Pausing by a painting of one of the ranch's studs, she met Devon's gaze. "Which makes you wonder how she learned about it in the first place."

"I didn't question her methods." He scrubbed a hand through his hair, frustrated. "With everything it's taking to get the launch event off the ground, I really need April to do her job so I can take care of mine."

Moreover, as much as he wanted answers for Regina's sake, he wasn't in that much of a hurry for the truth to come tumbling out before his mother's wedding.

Not that Regina would necessarily run to the tabloids to share the news. But what if she decided to do just that?

"Maybe it's time we give April some backup." She picked up her purse again, a new spark of determination in her eyes as she hooked the strap over her shoulder. She looked like a woman ready to head out the door again.

"What do you mean?" Wariness crept through him even as he grabbed his keys from a hook near the kitchen counter.

"April Stephens has the best lead yet on your father's secrets." Regina was already moving toward the coat rack to retrieve her parka and gloves. "And while *her* hands might be tied with how hard she can push her sources as a professional investigator, mine are not."

"Just because you ask her to reveal her sources doesn't mean she will." He took the coat from her to help her into it, tugging her hair from the collar. "That could be proprietary information."

He didn't want their evening together to end, but he didn't plan on standing in her way when she was on fire to get answers to her questions. Even if that meant he had to face more hard truths about his father, the man he'd never known as well as he'd thought. The facts needed to come out before either of them could find peace. He'd bring her back to the bunkhouse and then figure out his next move.

As much as he didn't want to call his brother in Paris let alone admit Alonzo's murky past was proving tough to investigate, Devon wondered if he should give Marcus a heads-up about what April had discovered so far. Devon's longtime rivalry with his half brother needed to end if they were going to present a united front when the truth about Alonzo was revealed.

He hadn't wanted to believe his father was involved in anything illegal, but considering the lengths Alonzo had gone to in order to keep his secrets, it sure made Devon wonder.

"If April has run out of options for shaking more information free from her source, she might be glad for a new approach." Regina tugged on her gloves and studied him with a level gaze. "I got the impression that April has a lot riding on this case, too."

Devon thought back to his meeting with April Stephens. She'd been professional. Thorough. Committed. But he hardly got the impression she had anything personal at stake.

Not like they did.

Regina reached for the door, but he put his hand over hers, needing to slow things down. The feel of her sent a bolt of desire through him, but he restrained himself for now.

"I'm not so sure about that," he told her. "But I can promise you we're going to have answers sooner or later."

He didn't miss the shadows that passed through Regina's eyes as she stared back at him.

"It has to be sooner." She threaded her fingers through his, her touch as urgent as her tone. "I've been waiting far too long for answers already."

Worry gnawed at him as he opened the door and escorted her out into the snow. Regina was desperate for her quest to yield information. Now.

And more than anything, Devon needed time. To get past his mother's wedding, for damn sure. But maybe more important, he needed time to figure out why Regina had so thoroughly rocked his world and what the hell he was going to do about it.

Ten

Regina retreated to her trusty laptop, the same way she had for years every time she heard about a new piece of information that might finally solve the puzzle of why someone would write a book that ruined her life.

After she'd said good-night to Devon, she slipped into the bunkhouse bathroom and changed into flannel pajama pants and a long-sleeved thermal T-shirt. Combing through her hair—tangled from lovemaking—she couldn't help but feel a twinge of regret that the need to research the clues had sent her fleeing Devon's arms for the night.

She'd had a good evening with him. No, that didn't do their date justice. She'd had a special, amazing time decorating the tree with him and then retreating to his bed, where their sensual connection had blazed into a bond she would have never expected to feel for her enemy's son.

And that left her feeling more than a little unsettled. Confused. Full of what-ifs... Most of all, what if they'd met on even, uncomplicated ground.

Turning from the mirror, she emerged from the bathroom to retrieve her laptop, telling herself not to dwell on a relationship that could never go farther than this time together in Montana. Devon's launch event and his mother's wedding were both less than a week away, and as soon as everything was over, he'd be on a flight back East.

Without her.

She tucked her brush into her toiletries bag and hung her wrinkled clothes in the nook near her bed, trying not to think about how much that might hurt. They hadn't known each other long, after all. And yet he'd become more important to her faster than anyone she'd ever known. Who else had taken up her cause for answers the way Devon had this week? He hadn't protested when she'd left his cabin tonight. He'd understood her need to dig deeper for answers about his father.

Her gaze went to her laptop in its neoprene case at the bottom of her drawer, and she withdrew it slowly, thinking about all the times *Hollywood Newlyweds* had robbed her of real-life experiences. She still ached over how the book had fractured her family life, robbed her of friendships and nearly cost her

her life in the car wreck. Therapy had helped, but she still hadn't found the peace she so desperately needed. And now she was spending her time picking apart the mystery of the author and his motives when she could be lounging in bed with a gorgeous, successful businessman who genuinely seemed to care about her.

How much more would she let the book steal from her?

Behind her, she heard the floorboards creak and turned to see Millie wander in with a steaming mug in one hand and a paperback novel in the other.

"Hey, hon," the older woman greeted her, laying the book on an unused bed. A kitschy reindeer cocktail ring clanked against her stoneware mug as she wrapped both hands around the cup as if to keep her fingers warm. "How was your date?"

Regina smiled over how Millie had remembered she was seeing Devon tonight and cared enough to ask how it went. Touched, she set down the laptop and leaned her hip into the ladder on the sturdy built-in bunks.

"It's hard to say." She breathed in the scent of hot cocoa, soaking in the joy of a friendship from an unexpected source. "We had a great time decorating a tree and…" Her cheeks warmed. "Um. Getting close."

A wicked twinkle glowed in Millie's eyes. "Sounds fun. Which begs the question, what are you doing back home already?"

Was it a burning need to do April Stephens's investigative work for her? Or was there more to it than that?

"I thought I had a good reason." She'd attended enough counseling sessions to identify an attempt to rationalize her choices. "But I'm wondering now if it was old trust issues that sent me running."

Frowning, Millie took a sip of her cocoa before responding. "It's always a risk trusting people— friends, parents, coworkers…romantic interests."

"There's a high potential for hurt in those relationships." Regina should know. She'd been kicked in the teeth by life enough times to have all the survival badges. "Is it so wrong to want to spare myself that pain? To just have fun?"

Mille tilted her head to one side, her steel-gray ponytail swinging down. "But are you having fun?"

No.

She was mostly having stress.

"Sort of," she said finally, smoothing her hand over the peacock blue quilt on her bed. Her maternal grandmother had given it to her long ago, and the pattern was "double wedding ring." A romantic name for a pretty design. A dream that seemed far out of reach for her, considering her parents' spectacular failure and her experience with rejection. "I mean, I had fun tonight."

"And maybe that will be enough." Millie patted her shoulder, a brief, comforting touch. But as the silence between them stretched, she added, "Just keep in mind that if you always play it safe with people,

you might miss out on the chance for deeper connections that can lead to something really wonderful."

Regina knew she could never put herself on the
line that way with Devon. There was zero chance that
their out-of-control attraction would lead to something "deeper." It was amazing they'd already found
as much common ground as they had. Because even
if she ignored the way the book put them at odds,
they were still very different people. Devon was an
entrepreneur with a company on the verge of international expansion and she was drifting through different jobs while she chased her dream of payback.

Regina hadn't even really figured out what to do
with her life once she put the ghosts of the past to
rest. Devon had a family to go home to back East.
She was untethered, isolated from the only family
she had left. Her real father didn't have room for her
in his life, while she and her mother had never really
put their relationship back together again.

"Perhaps you're right." Regina wondered how she
could move forward with her mom. Put the past behind them for good.

"Just remember to take some risks now and then,"
Millie encouraged her, warming to her topic and gesturing as she spoke, the crystals on her reindeer ring
flashing in the glow from a pendant light. "None of
us goes through life unscathed. We're all going to
get banged up and bruised now and then, but that's
part of the ride, honey. You take the risks to reap the
sweet rewards."

They talked a little longer before Millie went back

to the front room with her book. But the idea of taking chances stayed with Regina.

Once she was alone in the bunkhouse, she retrieved her phone and stuffed her arms into the sleeves of her parka before stepping out of the building into the starry night.

A light snow was falling as she dialed a number she hadn't used in a long time. She began to wonder if she'd get an answer when she heard a recorded voice and a beep.

Regina took a deep breath.

"Hello, Mom. It's me." She closed her eyes, wishing things were easier between them. "Call me back when you get a minute."

She didn't know if Tabitha would return the message, but Regina hoped so. She might not be able to smooth over things with Devon the way Millie suggested, but at least she could start rebuilding her relationship with her mother.

For now, it would have to be enough.

April Stephens had stalked men in her line of work before. A couple of cheating husbands in the early days before she'd specialized in financial forensics. Later, she'd tailed some business types suspected of embezzlement. Sometimes she followed potential leads who simply didn't want to talk to her.

None of those men had ever looked like Weston Rivera.

For that, she was grateful on her first full day back in Montana after her trip to Hollywood. The Mesa

Falls Ranch owner was so absurdly good-looking, she was distracted enough that she almost forgot why she was following him. She'd been trying to find the right opportunity to approach him as he finished up his work outside the stables, and somehow got caught up in watching him. Her gaze drank in the ruggedly handsome profile, the hazel eyes and longish dark blond hair, the powerful build and easy demeanor that let him handle the agitated mount he was leading around the snowy arena with a halter.

In the time he'd been working with the animal, the huge black draft horse had gone from pawing the ground and tossing its head to resting that same big muzzle on Weston's shoulder. She didn't know how he'd done it, but she felt as mesmerized by the man as the gelding clearly did.

When Weston broke the spell with a soft whistle, leading the equine into the state-of-the-art stables, April forced her brain back into gear. She wasn't here to ogle the man. Or to drink in the calming effect he had on her nerves as he moved around the arena. She needed to question him, since he'd refused to speak to her over the phone. And her professional pride demanded she have more information the next time she spoke to Devon. Although she'd uncovered something significant in her final interview on the West Coast, she knew it wasn't enough. Her client wanted the full story, and to nab that promotion she needed, she would have to provide it.

Now she waited a few moments before following him inside the building that housed the ranch's business office. There were stables on the main floor, with cobblestone floors and polished wooden stall doors. The place looked more suited to hold champion Thoroughbreds than working animals like the draft horse.

Brass lanterns hung at regular intervals on the heavy beams that lined a walkway leading from the foyer. April waited until Weston climbed the steps to the second floor, where double steel doors bearing the ranch name stood half ajar. Once he disappeared through that entrance, she trailed him, peering inside to where a reception area appeared empty. The scent of coffee hung in the air even though it was late afternoon, and she saw a pot percolating in the corner on a gray granite wet bar.

Beyond the vacant reception desk and a wall emblazoned with another ranch logo, a second door remained partially open. Weston must be in there. She could only see a glimpse of a conference table with gray leather swivel chairs.

She was sure she had him cornered now. He couldn't make excuses about his horse needing attention, or edge past her into the barn where guests weren't supposed to follow.

Striding into the reception area, she stuffed her gloves into the pockets of her long down jacket as she closed the office doors behind her. She was unwinding her scarf from her neck when Weston emerged from the inner office, his focus on a sheaf of papers in his hand.

"Hello, Mr. Rivera." She left her scarf dangling free around her neck, her jacket open.

He stopped short when he spotted her, his hazel eyes all the more compelling when they were turned on her. He'd removed his shearling jacket and Stetson. His well-worn denim and pale blue flannel didn't begin to hint at his wealth. With his dark blond hair brushing his shoulders, he looked like a misplaced surfer, right down to the bristle of a jaw he hadn't shaved for days.

"Can I help you?" His voice was deeper than she'd imagined. Low and melodic.

The timbre of it reverberated through her, resonating on a pleasing frequency.

"Yes." She wished they'd met under different circumstances, and she could have enjoyed the warm thrum of awareness. But since this job was far more important than the fleeting pleasure of a handsome man's voice, she came to the point. "I have a few questions to ask you about your aunt, Fallon Reed."

The look in his eyes went from warm and inviting to glacial in an instant. She could practically feel the chill of it.

"You're the PI who keeps calling me." He said "PI" like it left a bad taste in his mouth.

His tone was dismissive, as if he'd just seen her childhood home and the disaster area it had turned into these last few years.

She swallowed hard before she started again.

"It will only take a minute—"

"I have no legal obligation to speak to you." He

brushed past her and approached the coffee maker. Turning his back on her.

She watched him take a cup from an overhead cupboard and fill it from the stainless steel carafe of the high-tech machine. When the ceramic mug was full, he sipped it before striding back toward the inner sanctum like she wasn't even in the room.

Aggravated, she hurried to step between him and his office door.

"Is that really how you want to address this?" She suddenly stood too close to him, but she didn't think backing up a step would be a good move when she was trying to press him for answers. "Because if you're trying to protect someone you care about, don't you think a PI has more leeway keeping an investigation quiet than a police department?"

She was taking shots in the dark since she had no evidence that Fallon Reed had taken part in any remotely shady activity. But Weston's scowl at least indicated she had his attention.

Better she ticked him off than he ignored her.

"You have no idea what you're doing, do you?" He glowered down at her while tapping into her every last insecurity about her ability to do this job. "Or what's at stake."

Unease curled in her belly. Given his harsh tone, she wouldn't have believed he was the kind of man who could soothe a thirteen-hundred-pound beast if she hadn't witnessed it with her own eyes.

"I know enough to recognize that you won't want your ranch associated with a man like Alonzo Salazar once his past comes to light." She hadn't learned everything about her client's father, but what she'd discovered so far didn't paint such a pretty picture.

No one kept that many secrets without very good reason.

"He has a lot of friends who think otherwise," Weston assured her as he straightened. "And now, if you'll excuse me, I have work to do."

"You consider yourself a friend?" She stepped sideways to remain between him and his office. "Then why not set the record straight to maintain his reputation?"

Weston Rivera's eyes narrowed.

Later, she realized that should have been a warning. But for now, she watched him set down his coffee mug and his papers on the empty reception desk.

"I'm calling security to see you out," he informed her as he picked up the handset on a desk phone. Then he slanted her a sideways glance. "Unless you care to leave under your own steam?"

His gaze lingered on her a long moment. Long enough to make her feel a surge of awareness for him despite her frustration. Huffing out a sigh to hide that unwelcome feeling, she realized she wasn't going to learn anything from Weston Rivera today.

"I'm going to find out what Alonzo Salazar was up to one way or another," she informed him, wrapping her scarf around her neck again, if only to hide the rush of heated color she feared was climbing up her skin.

If he said any more, she missed it in her rush to

leave the office. She retreated down the stairs and out into the chilly wind blowing off the mountains.

Where she could breathe again.

Drawing in shallow breaths of crisp air, she tried to slow her racing heart. She feared she wasn't cut out for this kind of work. It was one thing to trace a paper trail from the safety of her Denver office. Being on the ground and mired in real detective work was far messier. Upsetting.

She'd had Regina Flores calling her repeatedly for the last twenty-four hours, wanting to quiz her about the investigation. And she'd fielded a half dozen messages from her mother's neighbors back home, threatening to take legal action if she didn't get her place cleaned up. April could manage it. She absolutely would get on top of it all.

Starting today, with a drive to Kalispell to confront Fallon Reed in person. She needed to make some headway on this case, not just because the job and the promotion were mission-critical to keeping her mother under her own roof. She also needed to see progress in order to experience the therapeutic effects of peeling away someone else's secrets.

That aspect of the job kept her working even on the days she didn't like it one bit. And if that put her at odds with the mesmerizing ranch owner?

She just needed to remember that she couldn't afford to get close to anyone anyhow. Her own secrets ensured that. No matter how much she might wish otherwise.

Heading for her car, she dialed Regina Flores to

start ticking items off her to-do list. She would take back control of this case. April had already sent the information she had to Devon, but she understood why Regina wanted to hear all the nuances.

The woman answered even before April heard the phone ring.

"Hello?" Regina sounded as desperate as April felt.

Maybe that was why she found it difficult to talk to the woman sometimes. She empathized a little too well with Regina's difficult journey. April remembered what it was like to have control of her life wrenched out of her hands.

"Hi, Regina." She hit the fob on the keys to her rental car as she approached the parking area outside the main lodge. "I have an update for you."

Regina had thought Devon's PI was trying to dodge her. But after a thorough phone briefing with April Stephens while the woman drove to Kalispell to interview Fallon Reed, Regina recognized that April had simply been too busy following leads to give updates.

Tucking her phone in her pocket, Regina went back to prepping for a bonfire happy hour down by the skating pond. She owed a giant thank-you to Millie and a few of her other bunkmates for pulling her share of the work during her phone call, but she was learning that was part of the employee code here. She'd covered for one of the ski concierges the week before when she'd ended up stuck overnight with a ski excursion. And in return, her coworkers had finished Regina's chore of lighting the antler Christmas tree they'd built out on the skating pond.

Setup appeared complete now, and the bonfire was lit even though the sun hadn't fully set. Regina could see activity in one of the dining rooms overlooking the skating pond. The waitstaff was preparing to bring cold and hot carts down to the ice so skaters could help themselves to cocoa, cocktails and appetizers. And, actually, as she peered up the hill toward the lodge lit from within, she spotted a conference suite where Devon was holding a meeting with the ranch higher-ups to finalize plans for the launch event.

Even at this distance, Devon was easy to recognize, from his broad shoulders encased in a custom-fitted suit jacket, to the way he leaned back in the leather swivel chair at the head of the table. His body was familiar to her. The way he moved. His gestures.

He would meet her at the bonfire afterward, and she was anxious to talk to him about the PI's revelations—that Alonzo had had an affair with her mother's yoga instructor, and the *yogini* had told him Tabitha's secret, effectively giving him all his story fodder. April hadn't yet figured out why Alonzo decided to write the story anonymously, but she'd asked Regina to weigh the possibility that he'd never meant for the story to be connected to the people it was based on in real life .

In other words, to consider the small chance that Alonzo had meant no harm with the book.

Boots crunching through the snow, Regina skirted the ice pond, remembering the unusual request, and how she'd rejected it out of hand. Why all the secrecy if he'd never meant for the truth to emerge? But the idea gnawed at her just the same, making her wonder what it meant if it turned out she'd chased down answers for years only to discover her life had been destroyed as collateral damage when Alonzo was only trying to tell a story.

But he'd done a poor job of disguising his sources of inspiration, and that felt damning to her. They'd know more about his motives, perhaps, once they could figure out where the profits of the book had gone, but April refused to share her information about the nominee service. Still, Regina knew they were getting close as her phone rang again. This time, her mother's number flashed across the screen, reminding Regina she'd been trying to reach her.

A mix of feelings washed over her. Nervousness. The old resentments. A tiny hope that one day they could have a relationship that wouldn't be overshadowed by the past.

Pressing the Connect button, she walked in the moonlight to the far side of the ice pond, where a gazebo provided shelter from the falling snow. She'd be able to see the skaters as they started to arrive. Devon had agreed to take a break from his work to meet her here later, too.

"Hi, Mom." Regina brushed some snowflakes off a picnic table under the gazebo before taking a seat on the wooden bench.

"Hello, Georgiana." Her mother's tone was cool. She sounded like she was in her car, or at the very least using her speakerphone. A rock tune played on a radio somewhere near her.

Regina bristled. "I'm not going by that name anymore, remember?"

"It doesn't change who you are, darling," her mom reminded her while a few car horns honked in the background. "And how's life in Montana? Are you honestly working at a horse ranch?"

Regina blew out a breath and tried to relax, remembering the whole reason she'd reached out to her mother in the first place. Hadn't Millie suggested she take more risks to build better relationships?

"I am." She'd imparted that much information in the message she'd left for her mother. Staring out across the ice pond lit with white lights strung from tree to tree around the perimeter, she couldn't imagine a more beautiful place to be right now. "It's peaceful here. I feel like I can think."

She hadn't realized how suffocating her life in Los Angeles had been back when she'd been trying to hold the threads of her unraveled life together. Back home, there had been reminders everywhere of all she had lost. The stores and restaurants she couldn't afford anymore. The parties that she didn't get invited to. And, of course, the tabloid interest in her story that made her feel like she was always running from questions.

"You needed *more* peace?" her mother asked drily. "I thought that's what counseling was for."

There was a biting edge to her tone, reminding Regina how much her mom had resented the discussions of her daughter's therapy. Then her mother sighed, and some of the bitterness eased when she spoke again. "I was under the impression you'd forgiven me."

Regina closed her eyes, trying to remember the things therapy had taught her about her family relationships. She had traveled this road with her mom before, and was unwilling to fall into the same conversational traps.

Her mom's answer to the upheaval from *Hollywood Newlyweds* had been to retreat. Ignore. Move on. But that had never worked for Regina.

"I meant a different kind of peace, Mom," she clarified gently. "It's really beautiful here."

In the long, awkward pause that followed, she could almost hear her mother debating her response. Finally, she said, "What drew you there?"

Encouraged that maybe her mother was going to work on establishing a new peace between them, Regina decided to be forthright. She spotted a camera crew setting up to take footage of the bonfire party as it began. It was bound to be crowded, since the ranch's lodge was now full to capacity as guests and media convened for the coming launch event.

"I think I'm getting very close to finally putting the scandal and that damned book in the past, Mom." Her thoughts had been all but consumed by the new developments since April Stephens had taken the case. Or—perhaps more to the point—since Devon had decided to spare no expense in looking for the truth.

His contribution toward uncovering his father's motives only added to his undeniable appeal. If only she could trust what she felt for him. Or trust *him*. She'd been putting up barriers with people for so long she wasn't sure she knew how to relate to a man any other way.

"That would be good news. But why do you sound so sure?" Her mother switched off the radio, a drum solo ending abruptly. "What did I miss?"

The curiosity in her mom's voice reminded Regina that this wasn't just about *her own* past. The scandal and aftermath had affected her mother, too. Had devastated her, even. Tabitha Barnes had never returned to Hollywood. She'd never acted in another film.

Alonzo Salazar had stolen Tabitha's secrets and profited off them, wrecking her life in the process. Wasn't it only fair for Tabitha to know the truth? She might have put her anger behind her—and the hunger for answers that haunted Regina—but that didn't mean she didn't deserve to know the truth.

"If I tell you, will you keep it between us?" she asked, needing to keep the information out of the tabloids. Not just for Devon's sake, but for her own.

"Of course," her mother agreed. "I learned the hard way not to share my secrets," Tabitha continued, a hint of bitterness giving an edge to her voice.

Relaxing a bit, Regina told herself it hadn't been a mistake to reconnect with her mother. They could mend their relationship, couldn't they? Maybe Millie had a point about taking chances. Deciding to start with her mother, Regina brought Tabitha up to speed on what she'd learned so far, confident that her mom understood the hellish ramifications of having the tabloids involved in their lives.

"Who the hell is Alonzo Salazar?" Her mother interrupted midway through the story. "Hold on, Geor—Regina," she corrected herself. "I need to pull off the interstate so I can give you my full attention."

Waiting while her mother swore softly under her breath a few times, conceivably crossing multiple lanes to find an exit ramp, Regina's gaze traveled back to the window where Devon was still in his meeting in an upper-level conference suite. Seeing him there, remembering how supportive he'd been of her journey—with no thought to the consequences for his own family—made Regina realize that the progress she'd made in her quest for answers wasn't as exciting as she'd hoped it might be. Somehow, nailing Alonzo wasn't bringing her the peace she'd expected because he'd just exposed problems that were already there just under the surface of her family dynamics. She just hadn't known about them.

Like it or not, Alonzo Salazar had only spoken the truth.

"Okay." Her mother's voice sounded sharply in her ears. "I'm in a parking lot and I'm ready to hear it all. Spare no detail, Regina. I need to know all about the bastard who destroyed my family."

A twinge of worry passed through her that her

mother sounded so serious about a topic Regina thought she'd put behind her long ago. Could her decision to share the news with her mom dredge up old unhappiness that Tabitha had put behind her? That hadn't been her intention. Maybe she'd just really needed to share the information with someone else—someone who'd been as affected by the scandal as her—because it was eating away at her inside to know the truth and not be able to talk about it.

"I'm telling you this in confidence, Mom," Regina reminded her. "I won't have the tabloids hounding us again."

"I know, sweetheart," her mother assured her. "I understand."

Satisfied, she took comfort in the words. "Thank you."

While she finished filling her mother in on the new developments in the investigation, Regina watched the camera crew film a few laughing ice skaters on the small pond, trying to reevaluate her feelings about the book and her family. It occurred to Regina that she was finally in the perfect position to unmask the author of the book that had ruined her life. She had a captive media audience. The storyline would be relevant since Alonzo Salazar had been a frequent guest at Mesa Falls Ranch, and his son was working with the ranch.

As tabloid news went, it seemed like a slam dunk.

It was an opportunity she'd been waiting for ever since she'd found the front door to her childhood home locked, her life as a pampered heiress—a beloved daughter—over forever.

Except, seeing the snow globe beauty of this place, seeing how her previously empty world had filled with friends and a warm, generous lover, Regina didn't feel the same thirst for revenge she once had. Because while she still wanted more answers about Alonzo Salazar's motives and where the profits from his book had gone, they no longer felt like the most important things in the world to her.

She'd placed all her anger on that one man—and things were more complex than that. *People* were more complex. Time to quit thinking of the past in terms of black and white and to see the nuances beneath. Her gaze flicked back up to the conference suite window, where Devon was passing his tablet to a colleague, pointing out something on the screen. He'd been so kind to her this week.

Even when she'd been spying on him and trying to wheedle information from him, he'd been supportive. So no matter how many issues from her past she dragged into this relationship, she knew he deserved better than what she'd given him in the past.

By the time she wound up her phone call with her mother, sharing more with her than she had in years, Regina felt ready to take a new kind of chance. A new risk.

And it had Devon Salazar written all over it.

Eleven

Devon's meeting ran long, making him late for his evening with Regina. He hadn't bothered to return to his cabin to ditch the business attire, or trade his overcoat for a parka, but at least he'd had a pair of boots in the utility vehicle he'd used earlier in the day. Now, as he trudged through the packed snow to where they'd agreed to meet, he could see the bonfire happy hour must have ended. The white lights over the skating pond were still lit, but the ice was empty except for a couple of antler trees twinkling in the dark.

He pulled out his phone to text Regina to apologize and see if he could still salvage some time with her. But before he could remove his leather glove to key in his password, a snowball pelted him between the shoulder blades.

Feminine laughter followed the ambush.

Tucking his phone back in his pocket, he turned to see Regina peeking from behind a tall ponderosa pine. She stood mostly in shadow, but the glow from the skating pond let him see her smile. The red ski jacket she wore was different from the dark duster she favored for riding. A white knit hat covered her dark hair. Seeing her stirred him so much that the feeling stopped him in his tracks. It made him nervous that she had that kind of power over him. He pushed aside those sensations to greet her.

"Hello to you, too," he said, closing the distance between them. "I'm going to let you get away with that since I'm late."

He wrapped her in his arms, pulling her against him for a taste of her lips, grateful to lose himself in the feel of her. This, he understood. He just needed to keep things simple. Enjoy the physical connection.

Even with the wind blowing off the mountains and a light snowfall swirling around them, he was all in for this kiss. More than any wind or snow, he simply felt the arch of her spine toward him, the give of her soft mouth under his.

"Very late," she reminded him as she broke away to look up into his eyes. She didn't sound upset, though, for which he was grateful. "I might need to throw a few more rounds at you to even the score."

"I'm sorry." He brushed another kiss along her forehead, wondering how she could feel so right against him. "With the party day looming, we had a lot of details to finalize. I didn't feel like I could rush through the conference call with the staffers doing the heavy lifting."

"I understand." She slid one arm around his waist and ended up tucked under his arm, subtly steering him toward a couple of Adirondack chairs flanking a firepit. "The one positive thing about being late for the party is that we've got a bonfire all to ourselves."

He'd rather have her in front of the fireplace at his cabin, where they could be alone, but he liked seeing her this way. She appeared happier than the last time they'd been together, when she'd rushed out of his cabin to dive deeper into April Stephens's latest findings.

"Sounds good." He followed the path around the perimeter of the ice. The catering staff was hauling the food carts back up to the dining area on the hill overlooking the pond. "Were you able to speak to April?"

He figured it would be better to dispense with the dicey subjects first so they could move past them. As they reached the stone firepit, he swiped off the snow from one of the seats for her.

"Yes." She dropped into the chair and leaned forward to warm her hands by the fire. "She was on her way to Kalispell to interview Fallon Reed and she got me up to speed while she was driving."

"I heard she didn't have any luck speaking to Weston Rivera." Devon had been receiving regular updates, too, and that one frustrated him. He took the seat beside her. "Which makes me wonder if the Mesa Falls Ranch owners are more tightly connected to my father than I first realized."

Peeling off her gloves, she laid them on the chair arms and held her bare fingers out to warm in the heat from the blaze. "I'm wondering if Weston said something to make April revisit her perspective on Alonzo. Because she asked me to weigh the possibility that your dad wrote the book without any intention of connecting to my family."

That was news to Devon. The idea sure as hell had appeal. He grabbed a nearby stick and poked at the logs in the pit, stirring the flames higher.

"What do you think?" he asked, dropping the stick to study her expression in the brighter orange glow.

"At the time, I said 'no way.'" She gave him an apologetic smile. "But I've been thinking about it ever since. And I know that it's wrong of me to pin all the blame on your dad when it was my mother who betrayed my family."

The pain in her words was unmistakable. He reached to touch her, to soothe her somehow, his hand skimming her back through her parka.

"But it wasn't his story to tell," Devon assured her, empathizing with how much it hurt to realize the people you loved didn't share your moral compass. He'd struggled his whole life with forgiving his father for how much he'd hurt his mom. "I understand that. Though I guess the book wouldn't have experienced the level of fame or sales that it did without that gossip columnist getting involved and going public with her idea that the story was based on real people."

"No one made the connection to my family for eight months." Shifting in her chair, she turned toward him, shadows chasing through her eyes in the moonlight. "Maybe no one ever would have if not for that columnist."

He wanted to comfort her for all the ways her life had spiraled out of control. He stroked her back, wishing his father had left more clear answers in the paperwork he'd left behind at the ranch.

"No matter what his intentions," she continued, dragging in a deep breath, "I feel like the time has come for me to put it behind me."

As the light snowfall picked up speed, she lifted her chin a fraction, and he saw the determined glint in her gaze.

"Really?" he said, feeling wary. He wondered what that involved.

"The biggest transgression was my mother's," she said firmly. "I've always known that, and that's why I started counseling, to try and work through my resentment at her. And my father was at fault, too, for just walking away. But even though I thought I'd gotten past it, I'm still here, spinning in circles looking for a way to blame my lack of family on someone else—anyone else—besides me."

"You've never been at fault—"

"Not moving on *is* my fault." From her pensive tone, she seemed to be at peace with the idea of taking full ownership. "I've seen that more clearly in my time here than I did in all the months I spent dragging myself through counseling sessions."

Weighing her words, he gazed at the skating pond, where the falling snowflakes sizzled softly when they met the bonfire's blaze. Then he turned back to her and searched her eyes, hating what she'd been through. His hopes for an uncomplicated evening together got more and more remote by the minute.

"That much I can understand. Being in Montana has given me a serious dose of perspective, too." He peeled off his gloves and threaded his bare fingers with hers. "As much as I want to support my mother at her wedding, I'm in no hurry to return to my grandfather's world, where everything is an excuse to network and get ahead in business."

Regina stared down at their joined hands for a long moment before raising her gaze to his. "Maybe it will be easier for you if I accept your invitation to be your date."

His heart slugged harder inside his chest.

"Are you sure?" He hadn't pressed her about continuing their relationship after this week, but he'd damn well been thinking about it.

A smile curved her lips. "Yes."

The light in her eyes called to him, making him realize how much he wanted to be alone with her. To spend more time with her. No matter what happened during the rest of their stay at Mesa Falls Ranch, at least he had that to look forward to afterward.

Edging forward in his seat, Devon captured her lips in a kiss. She sighed into him as her free hand wound around his neck, slipping under the collar of his overcoat to his bare neck just above his shirt.

She hummed a pleasurable sound against his lips, the vibration echoing through him and ratcheting up his need for her. It could be below freezing and he would still burn when she touched him.

"Come home with me," he urged her, scarcely breaking the kiss.

"Yes," she murmured back as the snowfall renewed its intensity.

Sensual hunger firing through him, he rose to his feet, lifting her with him, then peeled himself away. Blinking through the fog of red-hot attraction, he saw the same lust—or could it be more than that—mirrored in her eyes. Whatever was happening between them was moving fast.

As he led her to the utility vehicle on loan from the ranch, he told himself that as long as the fire remained purely sensual, there was no need to worry about it consuming them both.

But even as he opened the passenger door to help her inside, Devon wondered if he was only fooling himself.

Waking up beside Devon the next morning, Regina became aware of two things simultaneously.

First, she'd never felt this level of happiness in her adult life. Every cell in her body seemed to sing with contentment to be naked and lying next to this endlessly sexy man. He'd adored her from head to toe the night before, lingering in all the best places in between, until she'd drifted into deep, blissful sleep on a raft of happy endorphins.

Her second realization as the light of dawn streamed over the bed was that she'd never spent a full night with another man.

And as she examined that idea more closely, she acknowledged that was both strange and messed up. Somehow, she'd always found a way to distance herself from romantic interests, telling herself those guys in her past were never "the one," so it didn't matter. After the way her father turned on her, it wasn't easy to trust men. Yet her subconscious had quit blocking her from Devon, allowing her to enjoy the whole night in his arms.

Now, here she was. Naked. Happy.

And then realization number three hit: her heart was suddenly vulnerable.

Amazing how quickly realization number three could torpedo the first two.

Slipping from the covers, she retrieved her clothes to dress, worry spiraling out from that one thought like ripples in a pond. Millie had told her no one went through life unscathed. But was it so wrong for Regina to feel like she'd already had her cuts and bruises? She wasn't ready to take on more just when she was starting to let go of the need for revenge that had been driving her for too long.

She dug in her purse for enough toiletries to comb her hair and put herself back together, taking her time to try to steady her nerves, too. By the time she was ready to head out of the bedroom, she smelled the heady scent of coffee brewing and bacon cooking.

This man was too good to be true.

The feeling was confirmed when she first spotted him from the doorway of the kitchen. "How do you like your eggs?" he asked over the brim of a white coffee mug, the steam drifting up to caress his handsome features as he drank.

His flannel shirt was unbuttoned over his naked chest, his jeans low on his waist. Even after the supreme fulfillment of the night before, her gaze got stuck on the center ridge between his abs that ended in a sprinkle of dark hair above the top button on his jeans.

With an effort, she set aside some of the morning panic and uneasiness to enjoy his well-meaning offer.

"Over easy." Setting her purse on a chair in the living room near the cowboy-themed Christmas tree they'd decorated, she padded on stocking feet into the kitchen and helped herself to a cup of coffee from the pot on the breakfast bar. "You look decidedly comfortable in the kitchen for a man who grew up in a life of privilege." She realized how that sounded after the words left her lips. "No offense meant. I know I never learned to cook anything for myself until after my dad cut off my mom and me."

He grinned as he cracked the eggs into the skillet. "No offense taken. I had a brief notion that my father would let me visit more often if I was independent and didn't behave like a trust-fund kid." He shrugged as he tossed the eggshells in the trash. "So when I was about eight or nine, I asked our cook to teach me some stuff. And while my father never discovered my culinary skills, I've never regretted the lessons."

Eight or nine years old? She hadn't thought before about how his father's defection must have hurt at such a young age. Her heart ached for the boy he'd been… And the weight that he must still carry with him now.

"Consider me grateful to your cook." She helped herself to the cream and sugar he'd left on the counter. "And it must have been hard having so little of your dad's time growing up. As much as it hurt when my dad cut me off completely, at least I had him in my life until my midteens."

Devon shook his head while he dug in a drawer to retrieve a spatula. "I don't think anyone would say that the teens are an easy time to go through that kind of loss."

His words were yet more proof that Devon was a thoughtful man. Butterflies fluttered in her belly. She sipped her coffee to quiet the feeling while his phone rang. He silenced it with one hand and flipped eggs with the other.

"Do you have a lot of work obligations today?" She wondered about the schedule for the launch event. And their flight out afterward.

Last night she'd agreed to attend his mother's wedding with him, extending their relationship after the event ended. Her stomach knotted a bit at the memory. Not because she didn't want to be with him, but because of how very badly she *did*.

What if this risk exploded in her face?

Her belly tightened painfully.

"Yes. Although that message was from my mother, who's thrilled I'm bringing you to the wedding." His green eyes met hers for a moment before he plated the eggs and bacon he'd already cooked. "She's excited to meet you."

Her pulse raced at the realization that this was really happening. She was genuinely taking the next step with Devon, no matter that their relationship had started in such strained circumstances. Should she come clean about how she'd rifled through his jacket on purpose that first day?

She didn't want her first effort with a man who mattered to her to be marred by a lie going in. If she allowed that, she wasn't all that different from her mother.

The toaster popped near her elbow, startling her.

"You okay?" Devon asked as he set a plate in front of her and passed her a slice of toasted golden wheat bread.

"Sure." She nodded too fast. "Just realized I'm cutting it close to lead my first trail ride."

"I'll drive you back soon. I know we both have a lot of obligations today and tomorrow, but the day after that, you're all mine for the launch party gala." He took the seat beside her at the long breakfast bar, his green eyes turning a shade darker as his gaze smoldered over her.

She went from worried to keenly aware of him in the space of a heartbeat. How did he do that?

"I'd better start the search for a dress," she admitted, thinking how long it had been since she'd attended a black-tie event.

"I'm already on top of it," he assured her, straightening to dig into the meal.

"On top of dress shopping?" She gave a surprised laugh and nibbled at the bacon.

"You'll need a dress for the wedding, too, and I can't have you bearing the cost of that when I invited you so last minute." He tapped a screen on his phone to show her a web page for a well-known couture house. "So I messaged one of Lily's designer friends from New York to send you some samples."

Lily Carrington was his good friend and the COO of Salazar Media, who'd departed Mesa Falls Ranch after falling for Devon's brother, Marcus. Regina knew, because she'd spied on Lily and Marcus, too, in her quest to find answers about Alonzo. And despite the guilt that memory brought with it, she couldn't quite suppress a purely feminine rush of pleasure at the idea of wearing the gorgeous clothes he showed her on his phone. It had been so long since she'd had access to those kinds of garments.

"That's so kind of you, but—"

"I insist." He leaned over to kiss the back of her hand before returning to his breakfast. "I know the ranch has you booked for too many tours the next two days to give you enough time to shop. And for what it's worth, I appreciate your role in making this event a success."

She murmured her thanks before finishing her

meal, trying to sort through all the feelings swelling like an incoming storm. Was she moving too fast in taking new risks? She'd been so sure she wanted to pursue this relationship with Devon, but the closer she got to him, the more she realized how devastated she was going to be if things fell apart.

And no matter how much she tried to focus on the positives of what was happening between them, she had the weight of a lot of frustrating years riding on her back, whispering that it would never work out. Even with the launch party to look forward to—surrounded by friends in a place she'd come to care about—Regina couldn't shake the fear that she was one step away from screwing it all up.

Twelve

After all the hours he'd put in the last two days, Devon was more than ready for his night with Regina. The day of the launch event, Mesa Falls Ranch looked like a scene straight out of a kids' picture book. The holiday decorations were heavy on the greenery and red bows. Even the four-rail fences were decked with pine boughs, and white lights were strewn along the private drive that led to the main lodge.

An event space simply called "The Barn" was a historic reproduction in turn-of-the-century style, with a giant wreath decorating the cupola. The whole building was lit with landscape lighting in addition to the Christmas lights, making it easy to photograph for the wealth of camera crews present.

Fat snowflakes fell from the sky, giving every photo a snow globe touch. Dark draft horses in full dress tack pulled the sleighs conveying the guests from the lodge to the party venue, dropping them off on a red carpet that led through the huge double doors.

Inside, Devon had checked and triple-checked the logistics of the social media tech. He'd done all he could to make this night a success, and he wanted the reward of time with the sexy woman who'd dominated his thoughts all week. He walked past the massive screen over the dance floor already broadcasting live video feeds from the simultaneous party events in New York and Los Angeles. Here, the focus was on traditional black tie, but in the other cities, there were ranching gurus on hand to narrate programs about sustainable ranching. They'd flown baby lambs and sheep across the country in both directions to make ranching issues more real, combining petting zoo opportunities with social media content moments.

The intent was to drive awareness about the benefits of making ranch lands greener and establishing greater harmony with the animals—both the livestock and the native species. Marcus had brainstormed it, but Devon had executed the bulk of the events. Now, with everything running smoothly, he could focus on finding his date.

Leaving the barn, he stalked out into the snowy night again, checking his phone for messages. There were none. He'd called Regina ten minutes ago, thinking she was just running late, but now he was concerned since they were supposed to have met half an hour ago. He hated not being able to pick her up personally, but he felt it was important to be on site before the event kicked off in case the ranch owners had any concerns. Three of them were here tonight: Weston Rivera, Gage Striker and Desmond Pierce. Two others were attending the party in Los Angeles, and one had flown to New York.

Frustration spiked that this event had required so much of his time during a week he would have enjoyed devoting to Regina. And while he understood his brother's wish to take time with Lily Carrington this week, Devon knew it was past time to confront Marcus about the simmering rivalry between them. He refused to let it destroy their company. He'd worked almost nonstop since starting Salazar Media, expanding the business during explosive growth in the field. What was the point of all that work—all those profits—if he couldn't take the time to enjoy what really mattered? Maybe Marcus had already figured that out for himself.

Even as the thought crossed Devon's mind, he tried to push it aside. Because if he admitted that Regina really mattered, he would have to confront the fact that his father's behavior had soured him on relationships. That he didn't trust himself, considering what kind of male role model he'd had. He'd always avoided serious relationships because he didn't want to put any woman through the hell that his father had wrought for his mother—and other women, too.

He looked up, straining to see who the passenger was in an approaching sleigh. It wasn't Regina. Then he scanned the crowd for her face. He didn't see her, but as the sleigh pulled up in front of him, he glimpsed April Stephens in a dark blue gown with a high neck and long sleeves.

"April." He went to the sleigh to personally help her down. "Have you seen Regina?"

April's blond curls fell in artful ringlets around her face. Other men turned to look at her. She was a lovely woman, and yet she left him cold because the only female who captured his attention was a dark-haired beauty with quicksilver eyes and fierce determination.

"I saw her at the spa earlier today." April smiled as she smoothed her long skirt and rushed to the temporary canopy to protect guests from the snow. "One of her bunkmates had a couple of openings in her schedule at the pedicure station, so Regina invited me to get my toes done with her."

"Did she mention her plans for the evening?" He couldn't imagine why she wasn't here. Had she backed out?

He'd sensed she'd been nervous about attending his mother's wedding even after she'd agreed to be his date. At the time, he'd told himself that was only natural, since going to weddings and meeting families were traditionally big steps in a relationship and he'd catapulted them straight into both arenas when he'd invited her to his mom's nuptials.

"Of course." April laughed, a dimple appearing

in one cheek. "She seemed excited to go with you. She showed photos of her gown choices and let me help her choose."

Devon frowned.

So if something had gone wrong with Regina, it must have been after she'd seen April.

"Okay," he muttered distractedly, already straining to see if another sleigh was on the way. "Thank you, April."

Worried now, he was ready to ask one of the grooms about finding him a ranch utility vehicle when he saw one more sleigh headed toward the barn, horses trotting out in front.

She had to be in that one.

Waiting for the vehicle to arrive, he heard a commotion inside the barn—a subtle uptick in crowd noise as if they were reacting to a new band on stage. Or a speaker.

Which was curious, only because there was no change in entertainment scheduled for twenty more minutes.

He turned toward the barn, where one of the doors stood open despite the cold, thanks to the enormous heaters warming the space. A handful of people were moving purposefully toward the entrance as if something inside had captured their attention.

Curiosity turned to a bad feeling that something was going wrong inside. But he forced his feet to stay rooted outside for another minute so he could check if Regina was in the last sleigh. He waited until the horses pulled under the lights, where he could make out the faces of the occupants more clearly.

Regina wasn't there.

He began to feel downright dismal.

Had she blown off their evening together? Changed her mind about going to Connecticut with him for the wedding? Confused and still worried, he couldn't take time to hunt for her yet. Not when there was something clearly happening inside the barn.

As he jogged toward the entrance, he realized a hush had fallen over the crowd. In fact, as he stepped into the gala venue, he saw hundreds of guests in black tie all standing still, listening to a woman at the podium near the dance floor. Devon didn't have to crane his neck to see her; his company had installed a closed-circuit video system that was playing live footage from the three parties on a big screen.

Thirty feet tall, in full color, actress Tabitha Barnes—Regina's mother—had commandeered the microphone. She stared out at the crowd while she spoke, her gray eyes so like her daughter's.

"…and the author behind the book *Hollywood Newlyweds*, which ruined my life, has been unmasked at last."

Devon's gut sank to his feet.

Not just because an audience in three cities was about to know the truth that would ruin his mother's wedding. But because he couldn't deny how the woman had learned this secret.

Regina had betrayed his trust in the cruelest way possible. No wonder she was nowhere to be found tonight. She'd been too busy orchestrating the revenge she'd craved for years.

The sweet smell of balsam and cedar turned sour as he took a ragged breath. He stalked toward the control board, edging through rapt listeners to turn off Tabitha's microphone and the overhead screen and switch the channel to any other feed.

It didn't take him long to attract the attention of the logistics coordinator. He gave her the "cut" sign that would kill the audio, but it didn't really matter. Because Tabitha Barnes was already dropping her bombshell.

"His name was Alonzo Salazar, father of the social media moguls who run Salazar Media—"

Tabitha's audio dropped. For a moment, there was silence, heavy and thick with the shock that could only precede an eruption. His gut twisted in anticipation a second before the burst of reaction came from the crowd. Just then, the image of the actress on the big screen switched to a feed from the Los Angeles party, where a rock star known for his philanthropy was arriving to support the party. But the damage had already been done.

A moment later, the chamber musicians scheduled to play during the welcome hour returned to their instruments. The violins blanketed the buzz of gossip, muffling the details somewhat but not nearly enough.

"Salazar" was the name on everyone's lips. He heard it over and over like an audio recording on repeat as he moved through the crowd to confront Tabitha.

And, more important, her daughter. Because he knew without a doubt where Tabitha had gotten her inside information about Alonzo, and it sickened him. He was mad as hell—and yes, hurt—to think how easily he'd been played and betrayed when he should have known better. He would find Regina and tell her exactly what he thought of this stunt and her.

After that, he would focus on tying up his business in Montana so he could put this piece of his life—and her—behind him for good.

"How could you do this to me?" Regina wheeled on her mother in the hallway outside the restrooms at the back of the event space. Framed photos of the ranch's public buildings covered the wall, and there was a black leather bench tucked into the far corner.

Her mother had never messaged her that she was on her way to Montana. She'd simply texted Regina five minutes before her date to say that she was going to use the launch event as a way to "set the record straight" about Alonzo Salazar.

Regina had been devastated. Hadn't she explicitly asked her mother to keep the information confidential? Her mother had agreed. And still, Tabitha had betrayed that trust. Even as Regina had scrambled to stop her mom, she'd assumed Tabitha would attend the party in Los Angeles since that was right in her backyard—the family's old stomping grounds.

In a panic, Regina had called and texted her mom and her mom's friends. Then, when she'd gotten her first inkling that Tabitha had actually flown to Montana, Regina had raced around Mesa Falls Ranch like a madwoman in heels to try to stop the train wreck before it happened. Her feet were still freezing from tromping through snow in stiletto pumps, heedless of the need to walk on the red carpets laid out for guests. Her beautiful shoes and gown were ruined after she'd spent all day primping for this night, eager to see the look on Devon's face when he saw her. Instead of savoring that moment, however, she'd arrived with the hem of the plum-colored velvet sheath rigid with ice from her trek through the snow. But despite her best efforts to stop her mom, she'd failed miserably, not locating Tabitha until she was at the podium.

When it had been too late to protect Devon.

"How can I do this to *you*?" Her mother turned on her, narrowing her gaze. "Do you think you're the only one who has been affected by this nightmare? My life was stolen from me, too."

Tabitha paced the narrow hall in a floor-length emerald dress that was a size too small, a couture gown from a long-ago film premiere that Regina had once paraded around in as a child. Her mother's breasts swelled over the bodice, her now softer physique straining the side zipper. Poor dress choice aside, she was still incredibly beautiful on the outside.

On the inside? Clearly, she still wrestled with dark demons.

Regina could see that now with the perspective of time and distance. Funny how much she'd gained of both those things in her brief stay at Mesa Falls Ranch. Especially since she'd met Devon. She understood now that her mother's lies had hurt them both immeasurably. Not just recently, in breaking the promise to keep the information about Alonzo confidential. The pattern of lies was more deeply rooted, dating all the way back to Tabitha's decision to pass off another man's child as her own. Alonzo Salazar had done a great wrong in revealing a story that wasn't his to tell. But he'd been able to tell the tale because of Tabitha's decision to live a lie in the first place.

"Mom, I thought we were going to try to rebuild a relationship." She thought back to that phone call when she'd shared the information about Alonzo with her mother. She'd really thought it was a turning point for them, an opportunity to share the hurt and move past it. "But that requires trust, and after what you just did, I don't—"

"You're a surprising person to tout the merits of trust." The masculine voice behind her was familiar, but the tone bore an iciness she'd never heard.

"Devon, I'm so sorry." She turned toward him, knowing this was her fault. Hating that she'd hurt him.

Desperate to fix it.

And yet the remote expression on his face gave her pause as he stared her down. Dressed in a custom-fitted tuxedo with a sprig of holly pinned to one lapel, he looked achingly handsome. But the coldness in his gaze sent a chill curling through her.

Behind him, two burly ranch hands dressed in tuxes and cowboy boots stood at attention.

"Ms. Barnes." Devon's gaze flicked past Regina, landing on her mother. "There are still reporters out front. If you'd like more media attention tonight, I suggest you seek it outside the barn to avoid being escorted from this private event."

Her mother gave a harrumph of disapproval as she brushed past them both. Regina noticed how the ranch hands followed in her wake, no doubt tasked with ensuring she didn't return to the building. Not that Regina could blame Devon for that. Her empathy with her mother ended tonight. She felt only guilt that she hadn't stopped her.

"I had no idea she would show up here—" she began before Devon cut her off.

"We can speak more privately back here." He pointed down the hall, toward a small cloakroom located near a back entrance.

She noticed he didn't touch her as they moved together toward the coat check, and that made her tense with worry. A quick glance into the main area of the barn showed the gala proceeding normally, although a few heads turned their way as they walked past. She overheard "Salazar" spoken behind someone's hand. She could see the way Devon's movements—already brittle—tensed even more.

Dread for what her mother had done multiplied.

Devon spoke in quiet tones to the young woman working the station, and she stepped aside to let him pass behind her into the coatroom. Regina followed him, stepping behind three rows of coatracks to see an assortment of folded tables, chairs and catering carts. The buffer of the coats filtered the noise from the party, making the space feel private. The scent of pine from the log construction permeated the room.

"You have every right to be furious," she said as soon as they were alone once more, her nerves wound past the point of tight.

And maybe it was easier to speak to his back since she was intimidated by the coldness in his eyes.

"Perhaps I do." He turned to face her, his face a neutral mask. "But since anger won't fix the situation, I have no intention of indulging useless emotions."

She drew in a breath, needing to explain what had happened. To apologize. But he continued before she could gather her thoughts.

"Since my mother is about to be besieged by tabloid reporters looking to feed off this story, I need to be at her side for damage control." His gaze narrowed, coldly assessing her. "And to personally apologize for my poor decision to trust you with sensitive information gleaned by my private investigator. How much does she know, by the way? Everything?"

Regina closed her eyes for a moment. She couldn't bear to see his disappointment in her. She knew he was hurt, and she hated that she'd been the cause. She ached to realize how badly she'd messed up. She'd been so resentful of his father for tearing apart her family. But now she was the one to cause pain.

"Yes." She wrenched her eyes back open. "I

thought it would provide her the same closure as it has brought me." She had gained more than self-awareness these last weeks. She'd gained forgiveness. And that had been a beautiful gift she'd hoped to share with her mom. "I really believed we could put it behind us finally."

Devon's right eyebrow twitched, but his expression did not change. "Or else you believed you could finally have the revenge you've sought for years."

Crushed he would think that of her, she sensed there were far more emotions at work inside him, no matter what he said about not indulging them. She feared he was slipping away. That she wouldn't be able to fix this.

"I wouldn't do that to you." She'd grown deep feelings for him in a short span of time and she wouldn't just throw them away like that. She pressed her case, needing him to listen. "I didn't even know my mother had come to Montana until a few minutes before our date tonight. I panicked, but I thought I could stop her. With the benefit of hindsight, I can see I should have called you to help, but I didn't know she was *here*, in this state, let alone what she was planning. At the time, I was just so fixed on intercepting her."

When she paused in her diatribe, she peered up into his eyes and saw his expression hadn't changed.

A slow, dawning realization blindsided her.

"You really think I could stab you in the back that way, after everything we've shared?" Unshed tears pricked at her eyes as disbelief washed over her.

The anger at her mother stopped mattering. The

frostbite in her toes from running around the ranch in the snow ceased to be a problem. Because the only thing she felt was a pain knifing directly into her heart.

Devon said nothing. If anything, his expression hardened a fraction, his lips compressing in a thin line.

"You're cutting me off." The realization struck her as she quietly said the words out loud, and she felt the ground wobble under her feet. She reached for the closest coat rack to steady herself, her hand falling on rough wool and cashmere. "Just like my father did."

"No." Devon's eyebrows scrunched together as he shook his head slightly.

But it was crystal clear to her. Her grip tightened on the wool coat and the wooden hanger underneath it, her reality rocking along with the seesawing garment.

"You might not lock a physical door to bar me from your life. But you're shutting me out just as effectively with the coldness and unwillingness to listen." The strategy hurt her so much more this time. Maybe because she'd believed Devon was a better man.

"That's not true," Devon responded finally. Starkly. But since he didn't have any follow-up to the statement, she took it for what it was.

A knee-jerk reaction.

"It is, though," she said softly, straightening herself despite the pain in her chest, desperate to hold onto her tattered pride. "And I'm more sorry than I can say. For both of us."

Awkwardly pivoting on her heel, she headed to the closest exit, knowing they were done. She'd taken the risk and put herself on the line like Millie had suggested, but it hadn't paid off, because Devon didn't love her the way she loved him.

And she didn't have any idea how she was going to recover from that.

Thirteen

How could it hurt so much watching Regina walk away when she'd betrayed his trust?

Devon stood immobile as she strode from the cloakroom, achingly beautiful in her deep purple gown, half of her dark hair piled on her head while the rest cascaded in curls around her neck.

Maybe it pained him so much because she might be telling the truth? Had her mother acted independently of her? Had Regina only been guilty of confiding in someone she should have been able to trust?

And the most painful truth of all? That Devon had been no better than her heartless father, blaming her for something she couldn't control.

Except she could have controlled this situation.

She'd even admitted to telling her mom about the PI's report. Although if he could trust her reasons, Regina had said she did it in order to put the book in her past. For good.

Had she been ready to move forward with him?

Devon couldn't afford to dwell on the knot of questions or the cavernous ache in his chest. Not when he had an event to get through. And, far more important, he had to reach his mother's side to help her weather this latest Salazar scandal two days before her wedding, no less. Forcing one foot in front of the other, he began making his way back out to the party.

Swearing to himself, he paused near a stack of unused folding chairs to check his phone before he departed the privacy of the storage area. He'd already missed a video call from his mother.

His foreboding grew. Out on the dance floor he could see a few couples two-stepping, since the country band had taken the stage. He had to trust that his staff was keeping the event on track. Maybe his presence would only serve as a distraction since—inevitably—some of the media outlets would want a statement on the book.

He tapped the button to return his mom's video call, waiting in the shadows until the device connected. When the feed came through, he could see his mother on the other end. She appeared to be in the passenger seat of a vehicle wearing what looked like a cocktail dress with a heavy winter coat over it.

"Devon, I'm so glad you saw my message," she

said in a rush, her phone unsteady in her hand and making the image shake. "I wanted you to be the first to know what's happening."

He ground his teeth together, hating that she had to deal with the stress of his father's mistakes. And Devon couldn't dodge that he'd been a part of the cause for her pain by sharing the PI's information with Regina.

"Mom, I'm so sorry about that—"

"Sweetheart, there's no need for you to apologize." His mother cut him off. "You can't control the choices your father made. Besides, I think it's going to be for the best."

"For the best?" Devon asked, confused as hell. He tucked deeper into the storage area to focus on the call, gladly letting the gala event unfold without him.

A secretive smile curved her lips as she slid a glance to the driver's side of the car. In the background, Devon recognized her fiancé's voice.

"Damn right, it's for the best." At the man's gruff pronouncement, his mother laughed and glanced back down at her phone.

"Bradley and I have decided to elope. Tonight." She sounded genuinely excited. "We were getting ready for yet another one of Granddad's parties that turn into glorified networking opportunities when we heard about that actress's announcement."

From the other side of the car, Devon heard his mother's fiancé say, "And I said, to hell with it!"

Devon couldn't believe his ears. His mother was eloping? His grandfather would be furious. But if his mom was happy, that was all that mattered to him. Some of the knot in his chest eased a fraction.

His mother laughed again. She sounded sort of giddy. Full of joy. "I think Bradley was only too glad to have a reason to skip town. So we're going to Greece."

"I've said all along we should get married by a ship's captain," Bradley added, leaning into the frame quickly to kiss his future bride's hand. "We met on a yacht, right? This was meant to be."

Even when Bradley shifted out of the image, their clasped hands remained on screen, a silent testament to their solidarity. Trust. It made Devon glad because it showed how much this guy understood his mom.

Loved her.

Of course Devon was happy about that. But at the same time, seeing the way Bradley stood by his mother made him realize how much he'd just screwed up with Regina by not giving her that same kind of support when she needed it most. He'd shut her out. Refused to listen.

The pain in his chest worsened, a surefire sign that he had feelings far deeper for her than he'd been willing to admit.

"Mom, I'm thrilled for you," he said finally, grateful that she had someone looking out for her.

"I knew you would be." Her expression turned serious. "And I wanted you to know that there was no need to rush home to Connecticut for Christmas. Unless you really want to, of course."

She knew he'd never been close to his grandfather.

And he appreciated the heads-up. If he didn't need to help his mother navigate the renewed tabloid interest in her ex, he could stay in Montana for Christmas.

He had to apologize to Regina. Make her see how sorry he was for being so rash in pushing her away. He would do whatever it took to show her how wrong he'd been. He could be a better man than her father.

Or his.

Especially when it came to the woman he loved. The realization pierced through the muddle of his thoughts, the one, clear, burning truth.

"I think I'm going to stay right here." Devon was already moving toward the exit. He didn't care about the gala party without Regina at his side. Right now, he needed to find her and do everything in his power to make this right. "I look forward to celebrating with you both when you get home."

"Thank you, Devon. I love you, son." His mom blew him a kiss. "Merry Christmas."

The video disconnected and he shoved the phone in his pocket. He had to find Regina so he could share everything in his heart with her. Tell her how wrong he'd been and how much he loved her, how much he wanted her in his life.

And pray she would hear him out even though he hadn't given her that same courtesy. Just thinking about it made him realize how much he'd need a Christmas miracle to pull this off.

After changing out of her party clothes, Regina found herself back in the stables at Mesa Falls Ranch.

It was quiet there, with all the draft horses in their stalls for the night now that the sleigh ride portion of the launch event was done. The grooms had cleaned up well in the tack room, replacing the fancy dress tack on the hooks where it belonged. The scent of leather polish hung in the still air along with the sweet scent of hay. She'd been drawn here for the comfort of the horses after the heartache of the night.

After the betrayal of discovering that her mother was more interested in a media spotlight than in resurrecting a relationship with her. And the even more formidable pain of losing Devon.

She dragged in a sharp breath, stopping herself from dwelling on the memory of his cold rebuff. But the agony was still so fresh. The heartbreak so devastating. She caught sight of her reflection in a shiny halter plate bearing one of the horse's names. The woman's face staring back at her was growing more familiar as Regina Flores became more real to her.

For all the hurts she'd experienced tonight, Regina was still standing. Not fragile Georgiana Cameron, the pampered Hollywood princess who'd lost the man she believed to be her dad. Not Georgiana Fuentes, whose birth father hadn't wanted anything to do with a daughter who reminded him of his mistakes.

But Regina. The woman who awoke from a car crash with a different face and a need for a name to go along with it. *That* woman was strong. And she was taking full credit for conceiving her, and for loving her. Because it would take all that strength to get over a heartbreak worse than she could have imagined. The heartbreak of losing a man who'd swept her off her feet in such a short time.

Leaving behind the tack room, she shuffled back into the stable to stroke the nose of Evangeline, the Appaloosa mare she'd saddled for Devon that day she'd taken him on a tour of the ranch. Memories swamped her, making her wonder how she'd ever sleep tonight without sobbing her eyes out.

She'd finally healed her past, only to be brought low by loving a man who didn't return her feelings.

"There you are." The voice startled her and Evangeline, too.

Hand falling away from the mare's soft muzzle, she turned to see Devon standing in the stable door. A tidal wave of complicated feelings threatened to knock her off her feet and drag her under. She tipped her forehead to the horse's cheek, taking strength from the animal's calming presence.

Devon cast a shadow over her since the only light she'd flicked on was a lantern near the entrance. He still wore his tuxedo from the party, though he now wore boots and a long duster over it. Snowflakes dusted the dark coat, and he stamped his boots to free them of icy bits.

"Here I am." She smiled sadly, unsure why Devon would seek her out but hoping she could hold back her emotions and save her pride if not her heart. "In the last place I thought I would see you." She hadn't wanted to run into him again before he left for his mother's wedding. Especially since she was supposed to have been accompanying him. She'd told all her bunkmates that she was leaving for the Christmas holiday. "You're going to miss your flight if you don't hurry."

"I'm not going to Connecticut." He hovered near the entrance, not getting closer, but not leaving, either. "My mother decided to elope instead."

Regina exhaled hard, twinges of guilt stinging her over the woman losing out on her special day. The news did little to alleviate her guilt. But then again, she hadn't been the one to hold an impromptu press conference during the launch event, so why should she bear that weight? She'd done her best to stop her mother.

"I've already apologized, but please know if this elopement has to do with my mother's announcement, I'm sorry for—"

"I know." He hung his head for a moment before taking a step closer to her. "And I'm sorry I was too much of a stubborn ass to listen to you then."

Now that caught her attention.

While it was hardly enough to soothe a broken heart, she liked to think maybe he knew how hurtful he'd been. She leaned on the wall between stalls, not trusting her shaking legs to hold her upright. "I'm listening."

"Regina, it was wrong of me to assume the worst of you." Peeling off his gloves, he took another step closer. Close enough that she could see what looked like genuine anguish scrawled across his handsome features. "You gave me no reason to doubt you, and I got defensive right away."

She folded her arms across her chest to hold in the pain of the memory, needing to hear more from him before jumping in with both feet again.

"I'm done being judged based on the actions of my mother." She had thought she'd moved past the old tensions with her mom after the counseling sessions, but apparently, she'd needed this reminder to understand that sometimes you couldn't trust people who were supposed to love you. "I really thought she and I could resurrect a relationship, but tonight proved to me how wrong I was. And that hurts."

"I hate knowing that I only added to your grief after that painful realization." He stepped closer once more, bringing him within reach. He lifted a hand to touch her shoulder, his grip gentle and warm. "I don't expect you to forgive me for the way I behaved, but I had to find you to tell you how much I regret it. How sorry I am."

Hearing the heartfelt apology eased her misery a little. The physical contact helped, too, although she didn't dare let herself think there was anything more at work here than just that olive branch. She'd been through enough tonight.

"I appreciate you finding me and telling me that," she said, the words sounding stiff and formal since she couldn't let her guard down. Her gaze landed on his boots, which she now realized looked frozen. Her attention shifted back to his face. "How *did* you find me?"

"By looking everywhere. This was the last building on my list, but I saved it for the end so I could get a horse and start riding the trails if I didn't find you anywhere else. That was my next guess—that you took off on horseback."

"I thought about it," she admitted, feeling begrudgingly moved that he'd searched the grounds for her personally.

In a tuxedo. In December.

His hand on her shoulder was softening her defenses, his caress reminding her how much this man affected her.

"I should have come here sooner. I remember you saying how much you missed the Arabian of your youth, and that's why you wanted to keep this job." He shook his head. "But I ignored my instincts, thinking I should search the ranch more methodically."

It heartened her that he remembered her talking about the horse she'd had as a teen. She felt herself melting, hoping.

"You're a good listener," she acknowledged. "Most of the time. And, for what it's worth, I do understand what it's like to be so rattled you make poor decisions. I know it had to be awful to hear my mom at the podium tonight."

His green eyes tracked hers as he lifted his hand to her face.

"Nothing was as awful as losing you." The words stroked over her as tenderly as his touch. "Nothing else even came close."

Her heart pounded faster at the admission, a fragile hope taking root while Evangeline nuzzled the back of her shoulder.

"You seemed content enough with your decision when I left the gala." It had taken all her strength to walk away with her head held high. Where was he going with this?

"I never gave myself a chance to trust a relationship, in light of the twisted role model I had." His thumb brushed her cheek and she couldn't bring herself to pull away. "I told myself our connection was just physical, even when my heart knew there was far more to it than that."

She knew it, too. But hearing him say it, seeing the truth in his eyes, swept away the last of her pain and opened her heart to beautiful possibilities she hadn't dared to entertain before now. Before Devon.

"What made you change your mind?" she asked, still needing to hear the reasons.

He sounded more certain of himself this time. Outside the stables, a gust of wind battered the windowpanes, reminding her how cold the night had turned.

"My mother and I had a video chat." He reached to stroke the horse's muzzle as the Appaloosa nosed closer to them. "She told me she was eloping. She was already in the car with her fiancé, and they were going to catch a plane to Greece to get married by a ship's captain."

"That sounds wildly romantic." She was happy for his mother. Relieved that her mom hadn't totally wrecked the wedding plans with her ploy for media attention.

"It is. Even though the wedding plans were going up in smoke, she still seemed so happy they were together, because her fiancé turned a tough situation around for her." His brow furrowed as his focus turned on her, the truth of his emotions plain to see. "Seeing that bond, the unshakable connection, really slammed home how I'd failed you when you needed me."

Her throat burned with emotions as he shared the memory with her. She blinked through the feelings, not quite sure where it was all leading, but hoping desperately that his being here meant he wanted to fix things. Try again. She couldn't speak over the lump in her throat.

"More than that, Regina," he continued, his eyes locking on hers in the shadowy light cast by that single brass lantern, "it made me realize how much I wanted to bring you that kind of happiness. It made me understand that I love you."

The words reverberated as if he'd shouted them, even though he'd never raised his voice. The echoes of that simple, incredible statement burrowed deep into her heart. Her soul.

Unable to hold back another moment, she flung her arms around him and buried her face against his chest to feel the warmth of him against her. The scent of the holly berry sprig on his tuxedo lapel mingled with a hint of his aftershave, familiar to her after the nights spent in his arms. In his bed. She breathed him in along with his love as he kissed the top of her head.

When she had soaked up his strength, and reminded herself he was real—that all of this was real—she edged back to look up at him.

"Does that mean you forgive me?" he asked, his voice a raw whisper that revealed how much he meant what he'd said.

"Yes." Knowing how important this was to him soothed every hurt in her soul. "It also means that I love you, too, and it stole my breath that you feel the same way."

He bent to kiss her lips. The long and lingering kiss stirred her more than ever with the strength of this love firing through them.

"Everything else we can fix," he vowed as he pulled back to look at her. "I promise I'll never hurt you like that again."

"I'm trusting you." She remembered how Millie told her that you take risks to reap the sweet rewards. She couldn't imagine a sweeter feeling in the world.

"I'm going to make sure you never regret it." He wrapped her in his arms, making her feel safe. Loved. Desired.

She arched up to kiss him again, her heart and thoughts full of joy over how she could look forward to repeating the pleasure.

"What are you doing for Christmas?" she asked, ready to have him all to herself for the night. "Because I have some free time I could spend with you before I have to be back at work."

"The cabin is mine for the rest of the week," he mused, a glint in his eyes. "And the tree is already decorated. I have an excellent idea for how we should spend the holidays, just you and me. Together."

"Perfect." Contentment curled around her. She would be able to see her friends, who'd become like family. But most important, she could be with Devon to plan for a future. "We can have a cowboy Christmas."

Epilogue

Two months later

"This view is so gorgeous."

Devon heard the awe in Regina's voice as she emerged from the bedroom to peer out the living area's bay window in the luxury cabin he'd rented them for the week. Glacier National Park sprawled before them, the cloudless blue sky making the mountains stand out in sharp relief above Saint Mary Lake.

"I'm looking at an even better one," he assured her, rising from the sofa where he'd been waiting for her to dress for an early dinner.

She took his breath away, the same way she had

since they'd first met. For the last two months, she'd allowed her hair to return to its natural color, a pale blond that made her gray eyes all the more dramatic. She didn't seem concerned with hiding who she was anymore, even with the media's renewed interest in her family. But she also seemed content to leave her identity as Georgiana behind. Tonight, with a diamond ring in the pocket of his jacket, he hoped she would consider taking a new last name, as well.

She'd chosen an amethyst-colored sweater dress that hugged her curves and sky-high gray heels that showed off beautiful legs. But the best part of this outfit was her contented smile, a radiant happiness he liked to think he'd helped to put there.

The investigation into his father's past continued—privately, thanks to April Stephens—but Regina seemed content to wait for answers about why he'd written his book and where the profits went.

"You are completely biased," she teased, turning toward him. A pair of heart-shaped diamonds that he'd given her for Valentine's Day dangled from her ears. "But thank you just the same."

"I'm a lucky, lucky man." He folded her in his arms, drawing her against him to savor the feel of her.

In the months since Christmas, they'd never gone more than three days apart, even though she'd wanted to stay on at Mesa Falls Ranch for a while to find her footing again. He'd respected that, knowing how much she enjoyed the horses and the sense of family she'd gained from the friends she'd made there—something she hadn't experienced since her youth.

But he'd brought her to New York on her days off, showing off the city to see what she thought, since his work was based there. His mom adored her, and had lobbied for her to move closer so they could see each other more, an invitation Regina seemed to be seriously considering. He'd move anywhere to make her happy, and find a way to do his job wherever he was now that he and Marcus had decided the only path forward for Salazar Media was to keep the company together. To continue to run it as a team. The decision felt right now that they both understood brotherhood didn't have to be a competition. They could succeed together.

So Devon could work on the West Coast or in New York, and it didn't matter to him. Yet Regina genuinely enjoyed Manhattan, delighting in the luxuries that the city could provide. Tonight, he was going to see what she thought about a farm upstate where they could keep horses and he could commute in a few days a week.

If she didn't love that idea, he could see about setting up a presence in Montana, because this place would always hold a piece of his heart for bringing this woman into his life.

"I hope you still feel lucky now that your girlfriend is officially unemployed." She arched an eyebrow at him. "It seemed strange to pack up my things from Mesa Falls yesterday."

"I know it wasn't easy." He understood that she

was more attached to the friendships than anything else. But he also wanted her to find whatever path in life brought her the most joy, and he had the feeling she was getting ready for her second act now that she'd put her past to rest. "But Millie said she'd come and see you no matter where you end up."

They'd talked about taking time off—together—to travel for the next two months. See new places. Explore the world. Find out what made them happiest. Marcus—already a married man since he'd tied the knot in Paris on New Year's Eve—had been supportive, assuring him the company would survive without him for eight weeks.

Devon hoped he would be as fortunate as his brother. He couldn't wait to ask Regina to be his wife.

"I know." Regina rested her head against his shoulder for a long moment, gazing out the window with him. "It's up to me to figure out what to do next."

"Are you okay with that?" He tipped her face up to his. "I know there's been a lot of change in the last few months. But I'll move mountains to make you happy."

He'd already helped her navigate a meeting with her father—the actor who'd raised her and then shut her out of his life. The guy had reached out twice after Tabitha's announcement at the launch event, expressing his regret that he'd handled his wife's betrayal so poorly. But Regina had been open to talking to him again, and Devon had hope that the two of them—not related by blood, but by a shared bond and obstacles—would heal.

"I know you would." Her gray eyes met his, her fingertip grazing his lower lip. "And I love you so much for that, Devon. Thank you for giving me a chance to find myself again."

"You're the woman I've been waiting for my whole life." He felt it deep in his heart. In his soul.

He never questioned the direction of their path. All that mattered was that they took it together.

* * * * *

As the mystery around
Alonzo Salazar's legacy deepens...
Is Weston Rivera keeping a secret?

Find out as
Dynasties: Mesa Falls
continues in February 2020!

Don't miss a single story
in this must-read series!

The Rebel
The Rival
Rule Breaker
Heartbreaker
The Rancher
The Heir

by USA TODAY *bestselling author*
Joanne Rock

Available exclusively
from Harlequin Desire.

Get 4 FREE REWARDS!

We'll send you 2 FREE Books plus 2 FREE Mystery Gifts.

Harlequin® Desire books feature heroes who have it all: wealth, status, incredible good looks... everything but the right woman.

FREE Value Over $20

AVAILABLE THIS MONTH FROM
Harlequin® Desire

DUTY OR DESIRE
The Westmoreland Legacy • by Brenda Jackson

Becoming guardian of his young niece is tough for Westmoreland neighbor Pete Higgins. But Myra Hollister, the irresistible new nanny with a dangerous past, pushes him to the brink. Will desire for the nanny distract him from duty to his niece?

TEMPTING THE TEXAN
Texas Cattleman's Club: Inheritance • by Maureen Child

When a family tragedy calls rancher Kellan Blackwood home to Royal, Texas, he's reunited with the woman he left behind, Irina Romanov. Can the secrets that drove them apart in the first place bring them back together?

THE RIVAL
Dynasties: Mesa Falls • by Joanne Rock

Media mogul Devon Salazar is suspicious of the seductive new tour guide at Mesa Falls Ranch. Sure enough, Regina Flores wants to take him down after his father destroyed her family. But attraction to her target might take her down first...

RED CARPET REDEMPTION
The Stewart Heirs • by Yahrah St. John

Dane Stewart is a Hollywood heartthrob with a devilish reputation. When a sperm bank mishap reveals he has a secret child with the beautiful but guarded Iris Turner, their intense chemistry surprises them both. Can this made-for-the-movies romance last?

ONE NIGHT TO RISK IT ALL
One Night • by Katherine Garbera

After a night of passion, Inigo Velasquez learns that socialite Marielle Bisset is the woman who ruined his sister's marriage. A staged seduction to avenge his sister might quell his moral outrage... But will it quench his desire for Marielle?

TWIN SCANDALS
The Pearl House • by Fiona Brand

Seeking payback against the man who dumped her, Sophie Messena switches places with her twin on a business trip with billionaire Ben Sabin. When they are stranded by a storm, their attraction surges. But will past scandals threaten their chance at a future?

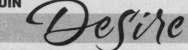

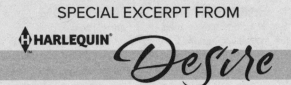
In the middle of topping up coffee cups, Jacob hesitated as a chill
rippled over his scalp. He shook it off. Found a smile.

"Wynn? That's an unusual name. I'm putting a case together at
the moment. The defendant, if it gets that far—" which it would
"—his name is Wynn."

"Wow. How about that."

He nodded. Smiled again. "So what does your brother in New
York do? We might know each other."

"How many Wynns have you met, again?"

He grinned and conceded. "Only one, and that's on paper."

"So you couldn't know my brother."

Ha. Right.

Still…

"What did you say he does for a living?"

Teagan gave him an odd look, like *drop this*. And he would, as
soon as this was squared away, because the back of his neck was
prickling now. It could be nothing, but he'd learned the hard way
to always pay attention to that.

"Wynn works for my father's company," she said. "Or an arm
of it. All the boys do."

The prickling grew.

"You're not estranged from your family, though."

Her eyebrows snapped together. "God, no. We've had our differences, between my brothers and father particularly. Too much alike. Although, as they get older, it's not as intense. And, yes. We are close. Protective." She pulled the lapels of her robe together, up around her throat. "What about you?"

Jacob was still thinking about Wynn and family companies with arms in Sydney, LA and New York. He tried to focus. "Sorry? What was that?"

"What about your family?"

"No siblings." As far as blood went, anyway.

"So it's just your parents and you?"

He rubbed the back of his neck. "It's complicated."

Her laugh was forced. "More complicated than mine?"

Shrugging, he got to his feet.

There were questions in her eyes. Doubts about where he'd come from, who he really was.

Jacob took her hands and stated the glaringly obvious. "I had a great time last night."

Her expression softened. "Me, too. Really nice."

His gaze roamed her face…the thousand different curves and dips of her body he'd adored and kissed long into the night. Then he considered their backgrounds again, and that yet-to-be-filed libel suit. He thought about his Wynn, and he thought about hers.

It didn't matter. At least, it didn't matter right now.

Leaning in, he circled the tip of her nose with his and murmured, "That robe needs to go."

Don't miss what happens next in…
The Case for Temptation
by Robyn Grady, part of her About That Night…series!

Available January 2020 wherever
Harlequin® Desire books and ebooks are sold.

Harlequin.com

WE HOPE YOU ENJOYED THIS BOOK!

HARLEQUIN® *Desire*

Experience sensual stories of juicy drama and intense chemistry cast in the world of the American elite.

Discover six new books every month, available wherever books are sold!

HDHALO2019

Love Harlequin romance?

DISCOVER.

Be the first to find out about promotions, news and exclusive content!

Facebook.com/HarlequinBooks

Twitter.com/HarlequinBooks

Instagram.com/HarlequinBooks

Pinterest.com/HarlequinBooks

ReaderService.com

EXPLORE.

Sign up for the Harlequin e-newsletter and download a free book from any series at **TryHarlequin.com.**

CONNECT.

Join our Harlequin community to share your thoughts and connect with other romance readers!
Facebook.com/groups/HarlequinConnection

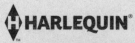

ROMANCE WHEN
YOU NEED IT